DRIVE ME TO ECSTASY

MONICA WALTERS

B. LOVE PUBLICTIONS

INTRODUCTION

Hello, Readers!

Thank you for purchasing and/or downloading this book. This work of art contains explicit sex scenes. It also contains elements of child abandonment and tense moments involving the injury of a child. If these situations are hair triggers for you and vulgar language and sexual lewdness offend you, please do not read.

Please remember that your reality isn't everyone's reality. What may seem unrealistic to you could be very real for someone else.

If you are okay with the previously mentioned warnings, I hope that you enjoy the ride this story takes you on. It will have you emotional, but most of all, it will have you feeling the love.

Monica

CHAPTER 1

K endall

THERE WERE some days when I loved my job. Then, there were days where I just wanted to say fuck this shit and move back in with my parents. I'd been a teacher for ten years and the beginning of the school year was always the hardest. I had to be the mean teacher to earn their respect, then lighten up a little as the year went by. The second week of school was no better than the first. The kids were extremely chatty, and I was tired as hell.

There was this one little girl, though, that I'd been keeping my eye on. She was dressed like a little boy and her hair was always unkempt. It was nothing to see that later in the year, but usually, at the beginning of the year, the little girls were all dolled up, dressed to impress. She was always clean. I could smell the scent of soap on her. Her dad always dropped her off at school, but another gentleman picked her up. I only knew that he was her dad because, one morning,

I'd had duty, and I heard her call him daddy. So, I really didn't know what to think of the situation.

I'd looked over her paperwork and there were only two gentlemen listed. The space for the mother was left blank and so was the space for the grandparents. It was really strange. Neither of them showed up for meet the teacher night and Cassie didn't attend class until the third day of school. She seemed to be extremely smart, though. After checking her records, I saw that she'd attended a school across town up until this year. I decided that I would send a note home to ask her father to call me or the school to set up a conference. Before she could get in line to leave, I called her to my desk. "Cassie, come here, sweetheart."

She looked a little nervous as she cautiously walked to my desk. Cassie was quiet and respectful. She was one of the good ones. I could tell that just the thought of being in trouble scared her. It was that very thing that made me even more concerned about her wellbeing. "Ma'am?"

"I wanted to put this note in your bag for your dad. Make sure he gets it. Okay?"

"Yes, ma'am."

As she walked off, I could see the sadness wash over her, so I said, "Cassie, you're not in any trouble, baby."

Her face brightened and I couldn't help but smile. Kids like her made coming to work every day, worth it. I tried to go over in my head what I would say when her dad called and how I would say it. I didn't want to seem nosy or accusatory, only concerned. As I contemplated, I saw one of the boys bothering Cassie. "Blake! I will send a referral to the office during the last five minutes. I don't have a problem with discipline. You better learn that! Leave Cassie alone."

He huffed. "Okay, Ms. Washington."

Right after, the aide showed up to walk the kids out. Thankfully, I didn't have duty today, so I could go home and have a glass of wine... or two... maybe even three. Two more days this week and it would be

Labor Day weekend. Thank God for an extra day. I packed up my things and headed to my car as I told random people bye and hugged a couple of fourth graders who I'd taught last year. By October, I would have these kids just how I wanted them... calm and receptive to learning new things.

Once I'd gotten to my car, I saw Cassie getting in the car with a gentleman. It was the same guy that had been picking her up. She looked extremely happy to see him. Maybe I was overthinking things. She didn't seem to be neglected. Maybe they just didn't know how to take care of a little girl. She was so beautiful. I just wanted to play in her hair. It was thick, like my natural mane and I could see how easily it could get unruly, but it didn't look like it ever got combed.

After getting home and sipping a glass of wine, I pulled out some papers to grade. Before I could even get started good, my sister, Alana, was calling. We were only two years apart and were the best of friends, along with my friend, Peyton, who we often called P. "Hello?"

"Hey, sis! What'chu doing?"

"Hey! Grading papers."

"Well, that won't take all night. You wanna go to the jazz club, tonight?"

"Alana, everyone isn't blessed to have days off during the week like you."

My sister worked as a teacher at the federal prison. She only worked on Mondays, Tuesdays, and Wednesdays. She'd been begging me to apply, but just the thought of being in a prison made me cringe. The money was better, and the schedule was less rigorous. But being around the impressionable minds of these children motivated me to learn as much as I could to help them, not only in academics but in life as well. "Pleeeeaaase, Kendall. P said she would go. We won't stay long."

I exhaled loudly. "Okay... ugh. I'll go. Let me finish grading papers, so I can get ready."

"Yay! And no spandex."

"Shut up! Bye!"

She was laughing as I ended the call. I loved spandex and so did my body. I had to be stuffed in boring ass clothes all week long, so when I went out, I liked to make a statement. *Damn.* That was what I wanted people to think and say when they saw me. People thought because I was a teacher that I couldn't be sexy. Well, they could kiss my ass. My job didn't define me. I finished grading papers, then headed to the shower.

~

"WELL, I see you wore what you wanted to wear anyway, bitch."

I looked over my tight, leopard print dress that showed off my tanned shoulders and cleavage. "Don't be a hater, Alana. It ain't my fault my body makes your ass and everybody's ass around us pause. Get over it."

Alana rolled her eyes as P joined us in the parking lot. "Hey y'all!" She looked me from head to toe and said, "Get it, sis!"

"Thank you, boo."

We hugged tightly, then made our way inside. All the tables were taken, and the bar was sewn up, too, so we stood around kind of grooving to the music. As we did, a gentleman approached us. Neither of us said a word and we were curious to see who he would talk to. Peyton had a boyfriend, and Alana had a guy she'd been kicking it with. When he stopped in front of me, no one was surprised. The problem was that although I got approached often, none of them measured up.

I didn't require much. They had to have a job, living on their own, and no more than two baby mamas. Drama was something I couldn't afford as an elementary school teacher. I couldn't have nobody coming to my job with bullshit. But hopefully, I didn't have that to worry about in this jazz club. *You could never be too careful.*

"Hello. My name is West. I just wanted to invite you ladies to have a seat at my table. There are three empty chairs. My friend that I came with dipped on me."

"Thank you, West. My name is Kendall, and these are my sisters, Alana and Peyton."

He nodded and smiled, then led us to his table. His smile was gorgeous, too. *Jesus of Nazareth.* The way he was dressed screamed style and class. We all looked at one another, making goofy faces, as we quietly followed him. I watched his tall frame pull out a chair, then he looked at me. Walking to him, I smiled, then lifted my hand, wanting to touch his beard. Instead, I gently laid it on his chest. "Thank you, West."

I could see the dark tint of his lips, so he was probably a smoker. He pulled out chairs for my sisters, then came and sat next to me. He licked those lips and I smiled. I wasn't easy by any means, but... the way his eyes caressed my skin was making me question that very thing. I'd been on a two-year drought. It didn't take much to make me horny. Just the way he was staring at me had my clit protruding. I turned my attention to the dancefloor and watched the couples dance as the live band got set up.

Jazz was one of my favorite genres of music, but I loved R&B, rap, gospel, and some pop. However, I would listen to almost anything once. If the beat caught me, then it was a wrap. I grooved in my seat to Boney James and Avery Sunshine as Alana and P talked. The waitress came to the table and I ordered a martini, then continued to groove until West grabbed my hand. Turning to him, I smiled. "Kendall, what do you do?"

"I'm a teacher. What about you?"

"That's cool. I'm a firefighter."

Well, damn. I could see him in a firefighter's uniform. He was fine as hell. I glanced at my phone to check the time. It was only eight, so we were doing good. Just as I was about to look away, it started to ring. The number wasn't programmed in my phone, but I remembered that Cassie's dad might be calling me. If it was him, he could leave a message and I'd call him tomorrow morning. I gave my attention back to West. "I'm sorry. How long have you been a firefighter?"

"It's okay. Twelve years. How long have you been teaching?"

"Ten years."

"Kendall, you're absolutely gorgeous. I haven't dated in a while, so this may be too direct, but I was wondering if I could get to know you more."

"I like direct, West. I haven't dated in a while, either."

His eyebrows went up as I smiled and slid my phone to him. "I was almost sure you were going to say you had a boyfriend. So, I'm pleasantly surprised."

He called himself from my phone, then slid it back to me. We continued to talk a little more, then he asked me to dance. West was such a gentleman and I was somewhat excited to get to know him. We swayed to the music and he complimented me on my natural curls, and I complimented him on his beard and asked to touch it. He nodded with a smile as I lifted my hand to gently run my fingers through it. It was softer than I thought.

Our eyes met as I pulled my hand away and I couldn't tear my gaze away from his. He'd obviously felt the same way, because we maintained our stare until the song stopped. West gently pulled me back toward the table, where Tweedledee and Tweedledum were staring at us with googly eyes. I slightly rolled my eyes at them, then sat in the chair I'd been in before we danced.

West and I talked and danced until I noticed it was ten o'clock. I had to go home and get some rest for tomorrow. He walked us out to Alana's car and made me promise to call when I got home, so he would know that I made it safely. "I'll call as soon as I get there, West. Thank you for keeping me entertained tonight."

"Anytime, and I mean that."

He lifted my hand and kissed it, then opened my door. As soon as he closed it and walked away, Alana said, "Y'all look amazing together. I hope this works out. You so damn picky."

"I am not! He already told me he has a job, so I'll find out through conversation if he has too many kids or lives with his mother. I didn't feel any negative vibes from him, though. That's a big ass plus."

Alana smiled as she drove to my house and I smiled. I was beaming from the excitement I felt on the inside. My instincts were telling me not to get too excited, but I couldn't help it. We seemed to vibe instantly and that rarely happened. When she got to my place, I hugged her and kissed her cheek. "Thank you for getting me out tonight. I had a great time."

"I know I pick with you a lot, but I enjoyed seeing you have a great time. Love you, sis."

I smiled softly at her. "Love you too, baby girl."

Once I got inside, I sat on the sofa for a moment, letting tonight replay through my mind. Retrieving my phone from my clutch, I called West. "Hello?"

"Hey. I'm home."

"Okay, beautiful. I know you have an early morning, so call me when you have time. I'm off until Tuesday next week."

"Okay. I will."

I ended the call and immediately saw the voicemail notification. Then I remembered that Cassie's dad had probably called me. Pressing play and putting my phone on speaker, I stood to walk to my room. "Hello, Ms. Washington. This is Price Daniels, Cassie's dad. I got your note and umm... I work during the week. Now that I have Cassie full time, it's really important that I work as much as possible. I'm only off one day on the weekends. However, most times, I'm available by phone. Thank you for your concern and love for my daughter. I'm usually up pretty late if you want to call me back tonight."

Hearing his voice caused me to pause while listening. It was a smooth baritone that lulled me into a trance, and he sounded very intelligent.

Unfortunately, I wasn't used to dealing with intelligence these days. Looking at the time, I saw it was ten-thirty. Surely, he wasn't still awake. I'd just wait until morning. I was glad that he didn't seem to take offense to my note. I'd simply stated that Cassie was one of my best students already and that I would like to discuss her grooming, if at all possible. I wondered what type of work he did to where he worked weekends. Continuing to my room, I started the shower and let my thoughts drift back to West.

CHAPTER 2

P rice

"WAKE UP, baby girl. It's six o'clock. Time to get ready for school."

When Cassie stood from her twin bed, I hugged her, then went to the kitchen to cook her some eggs to go with her pancakes and sausage. I tried to cook for her every morning, but my body was wearing down. This Sunday, I was gonna sleep as much as possible. The only help I had was from my older brother, Karter. Cassie's mama was in the wind. Cassie had stayed with me for our weekend together and her mama never came back to get her.

It had been financially taxing to buy her everything she needed. Her grimy ass mama was probably sack chasing. We argued all the time about her lack of interest in Cassie and I'd threatened to get custody of my baby several times. When she didn't come back to get her three weeks ago, I filed abandonment charges. I only had a couple of grand in my checking account and I didn't want to touch my savings. Getting things Cassie needed wiped my checking account out. My savings was strictly for buying a house. I was sick of these apartments and was trying to purchase a home. It would be more ideal for me and my baby.

I didn't know she would eventually be with me permanently, but this was where she needed to be anyway. My parents were deceased. They'd died in a car wreck three years ago. My brother and his family lived in their house and he helped with Cassie a lot. I didn't usually get off until around six. His daughter helped Cassie with her homework, and they fed her dinner. Karter's wife was white, and she didn't have a clue what to do with my baby's hair. I tried watching YouTube to figure it out, but I hadn't been successful.

Her teacher had sent a note and it made me a little nervous. I was hoping that she didn't think I was neglecting my baby. CPS was the last thing I needed to be worried about. Cassie wanted the cute girlie clothes, but the plain boy shirts were cheaper, so that was what I bought. I promised her that I would buy more girl stuff as the school year went by and I had plans to go shopping for her Saturday when I got off work.

As Cassie brushed her teeth and I scrambled her eggs, my phone started to ring. I frowned slightly, because no one ever called me this early. I grabbed the phone to see my brother's number. "Hello?"

"Hey, bruh. I won't be able to get Cassie tomorrow. I have to go out of town, and I won't be back until Monday."

"Okay. I'll figure something out. Thanks, bruh. Where you going?"

"Tricia's dad is in the hospital, so we're going to Jackson. It's not looking good."

"I'm sorry to hear that. I'll keep him and y'all in my prayers. When are y'all leaving?"

"Thanks, Price. We're leaving in the morning."

"Okay. Well, I'll check on y'all later. I need to make sure Cassie is getting ready for school."

"Aight, bruh."

I ended the call and scraped the eggs into her plate, then went to her room to see her putting her shirt on. Taking off from work was something I really couldn't afford to do. Maybe my dispatcher would have something for me to do Sunday, so I wouldn't lose a day of overtime. I hated giving up loads, but I wasn't going to have a choice. If I didn't, Cassie wouldn't have a ride home and she was too young to be alone.

Walking back to the kitchen, I ran my hands down my face and grabbed my phone from the countertop to call my job, but it rang before I could. It was Cassie's teacher. I exhaled loudly. Losing baby girl would kill me. So, whether this woman knew it or not, I was at her mercy. Didn't my efforts count for something? "Hello?"

"Hello. Mr. Daniels?"

"Yes."

"Hi. This is Ms. Washington."

I'd never met Cassie's teacher, due to work, but she sounded sexy as hell over the phone. Maybe it was worth taking off tomorrow to go meet her. "Hello, Ms. Washington."

"Cassie is the sweetest little girl. I wanna applaud your efforts. I noticed that her hair is always a little unkempt. Is there something I can do to help? Or is there someone in her life that can help with that?"

Hmm. She was offering to help. That wasn't what I was expecting. I relaxed a little, then sat on the sofa as Cassie came to the table to eat. "Cassie moved in with me the week before school started. Well... actually, her mama left her here. She was supposed to go back to her, but she never came back. As you can tell, I don't know how to comb hair, despite my efforts to learn. I have my brother, but there are no women in my life that can help."

"Don't worry, Mr. Daniels. Maybe I can help. Umm... this isn't as professional as I would like to be, but I will do anything I can to help my babies."

"Well, what time is your conference period? I have to take off work tomorrow to pick up Cassie. We can talk face to face."

Her voice was unraveling me, real shit. I had to know what she looked like. "Okay. My conference time is at one o'clock. So, I'll see you tomorrow?"

"Yes, ma'am. Thank you. Cassie is blessed to have you as her teacher."

"I'm blessed to have her. I have morning duty, so I'll see you two when you get here."

"Yes ma'am."

I ended the call and looked at my baby girl. Her hair was a mess. Maybe Ms. Washington could help us. Standing to go get dressed, Cassie looked up at me and I smiled at her. "When you get done, let me try to brush your hair, baby."

"Okay."

She was only eight years old, but I knew that she knew something wasn't right about how her hair looked. I felt horrible about not being able to do better. Once I was in my room, I brushed my waves and put on my boots. Driving eighteen-wheelers was always something I had an interest in, but now that I have my baby, I was wishing I would have pursued something more stable. My hours were everywhere, but I'd managed to land a dedicated run to where I knew what time I would start and around about time I would finish.

When I came out, I met Cassie in the bathroom. I'd been wetting the brush and brushing her hair that way, but that didn't seem to be too good. She had hair like her mama, which was a little coarser than mine. I didn't know how else to get it to stay in place. Doing my best, I brushed it backwards, then we headed out. I was gonna have to get some rubber bands or something to pull it into a ponytail with.

The apartment complex we lived in wasn't far from the school, but I had to be to work by eight and my job was about twenty minutes away. So, I had to drop Cassie off by seven-thirty to make sure I would get there on time. That wasn't too early, since school started at eight as well. When I drove through the driveway, I saw a goddess approaching the car. If that was her teacher, I was gonna let her help as much as she wanted to just so I could see her. "Is that Ms. Washington?"

"Yes, sir. She's pretty, huh?"

"Uuuh huh."

She was so beautiful. I was literally staring. She was mocha complexioned, and her hair was gorgeous. It looked to be in a natural state and her kinky curls were everywhere. She smiled and I stopped breathing. *Damn!* "Hi, Ms. Washington!" Cassie said excitedly, breaking me from my trance.

"Hi, baby!" She hugged Cassie, then looked at me. "Hello, Mr. Daniels. It's nice to meet you."

"Nice to meet you. Umm... do you have a rubber band?"

"Don't worry. I'll take care of her."

"Thank you. See you tomorrow at one."

She nodded, then smiled. *Shit!* How was I going to make it through that damn conference tomorrow with her looking like she was looking? I didn't know. But I *did* know that I would have to tame my thoughts, so she would help me with my baby's hair. However, if I wasn't mistaken, I thought I saw the same thing in her eyes. Like she was low-key attracted to me as well. I'd really be able to tell by tomorrow when we were one on one.

When I got to work, I went to the office to talk to the dispatcher. I didn't get a chance to call, because Cassie's teacher had called. Ms. fine-ass Washington. Entering the office, Crystal, the dispatcher said, "Aww hell. What happened?"

I rolled my eyes. She got on my damn nerves sometimes. However, I only came in the office when I had a problem. "I have to take off tomorrow. My baby won't have a ride home and I also need to speak with her teacher. If you have something for Sunday, though, I'll take it to make up for tomorrow."

She huffed loudly and I could have slapped the piss out of her. I worked my ass off and never turned down work. I didn't even have to work the weekends, but I worked every one of them muthafuckas without complaint. My daughter spent more time with Karter than me. Then it dawned on me that I wouldn't have a sitter for the weekend. *Shit!* Cassie was gonna have to ride with me, because I couldn't afford to take off again. "Okay, Price. I don't have anything for Sunday. So, you just gon' lose that day."

"Aight."

I walked out of the office before I cussed her ass out for that stank ass attitude. She knew I was her best worker, so whenever I needed to take off, it shouldn't be a problem. That shit rarely happened, but she knew the situation. I walked to my truck to pre-trip it, so I could go get loaded. Pulling tankers was the easiest eighteen-wheeler job, in my opinion. Sure, I carried hazardous material, but it was nothing to driving and sitting there letting the operators load and unload me at the refineries. It was easy money... except when the hours got long.

After pre-tripping my truck and I headed to the refinery to get loaded, my phone started ringing. I slightly rolled my eyes and put my earpiece on. It was against the law for truck drivers to hold the phone to our ear. Usually when my phone rang, it was because something was wrong. One day, shit would start going right in my life. "Hello?"

"Mr. Daniels?"

"Yes?"

"Hi, this is Ms. Washington, Cassie's teacher."

Shit! What had happened already? My heart rate sped up. "Yes, ma'am?"

"I know we are having our conference tomorrow, but I wanted to see if it would be okay to send you picture messages of Cassie. I did her hair this morning and wanted you to see it in case it got messed up later."

I exhaled. Shit, she could text me anytime she wanted to. "Yeah. Of course. You can text me anytime."

I could have sworn I heard a soft moan from her, but I was probably tripping. Shortly after, I received the text. "Okay. I just sent it. Well, I have to go. Have a great day, and see you tomorrow."

"Thank you so much. She looks so beautiful. Man, thank you," I said as I glanced at my beautiful daughter. "You have a great day also."

I said that shit seductively and wasn't even trying to. It was just that I appreciated her so much. My baby's hair was pulled up into a beautiful bun on top of her head and she looked so happy. When I stopped at the red light, I stared at her picture. I hadn't seen her smile that brightly since she'd been with me. She felt confident now and I could see it all over her. I smiled slightly. I owed Ms. Washington big time.

CHAPTER 3

K endall

"Ms. Washington, you have a delivery," the front office secretary said over the intercom.

"Okay. I'll be there in a little bit."

The kids were about to go to lunch, so I would go get my delivery then. I was so tired. The only reason I'd gotten dressed to impress today was my parent conference with Mr. Daniels. I'd stayed on the phone with West until almost midnight, before agreeing to go out with him tonight. We were supposed to be going to dinner and the movies. Our conversation flowed easily, and I learned quite a bit about him. He didn't have any children and he was a year older than me. West was from Lake Charles, Louisiana and had moved to Beaumont for work six years ago.

Even after the wonderful conversation with him, my mind was intrigued by Mr. Daniels. I admired him for stepping up to the plate and raising his daughter. It didn't help that he was fine as hell. I could see that while he was sitting. That smooth complexion, the color of perfectly baked cornbread... moist... soft... delicious. *Shit!* I had to reel my thoughts in before he got here, but his pink lips looked so soft and the way he looked me up and down, made my body shiver.

Just knowing that I would have to communicate with him often because I'd agreed to help with Cassie had me jittery. I'd combed her hair yesterday as best as I could, but today, I brought some product and styled it into twists that I pulled into a ponytail. I wanted to wash and braid her hair this weekend, but I was nervous to ask if she could come over tomorrow. This situation was so weird for me, but I'd taken so much of a liking to Cassie, I wanted to spend as much time with her as I could.

As the kids walked in a single file line to the cafeteria, I went to the office to see a bouquet of flowers. I smiled brightly, then retrieved them from the countertop. It was a beautifully arranged bouquet of roses and baby's breath. When I got back to my classroom, I pulled the card from the stem. It read, *I can't wait to see you tonight, beautiful. You are so intriguing and beautiful; this feels like a dream. Thank you for exceeding all my expectations. Until later. West*

I smiled, then sniffed the flowers. Grabbing my cell phone, I called him. "Hey, gorgeous."

"Hey, West. Thank you so much for the flowers. They're beautiful."

"You're welcome. I hope you aren't too tired."

"I'm able to function, but if I didn't have a teacher/parent conference today, I'd probably take a nap."

"I'm sorry. The conversation was just so interesting."

I could feel my face heating up. "What was so interesting?"

"Just you. Learning about you; the things that interest you. You said roses were your favorite flower, but you were more impressed with how they were arranged, so I tried to follow through with that. Knowing that you love music, especially jazz, made me smile. You have a brilliant mind, and you aren't afraid to speak it. I love that about you."

"Okay, you have me in here blushing."

"Then my job is done until tonight. I'll pick you up at about six-thirty. Is that cool?"

"Yeah. See you later."

I ended the call and sat back in my chair. My stomach was so uneasy, there was no way I could eat right now. After lunch was my parent teacher conference with Mr. Daniels. I'd never been nervous for a conference, but the fact that I was going to be asking for time with Cassie outside of school hours had me nervous. While West's words had relaxed me somewhat, the minute the call ended, my mind went back to the conference. After lunch, the kids would come back to class for an hour, then they would be off to PE.

"HAVE A SEAT MR. DANIELS."

He sat a bag on my desk as he sat in front of it. It smelled so damn good. My stomach growled. "What's this?"

"Just to show you my appreciation, I went to Charlie's BBQ and bought you a link. I hope you like it."

I loved food...period. How'd he know? My eyes met his. "I love all types of food. Who told you?"

He chuckled, then seemed to relax a little bit. While he was relaxed, I was still a bundle of nerves as he licked his lips. My eyes almost closed. I pulled the white Styrofoam box out the bag and opened it. When I opened the container, I had to take a bite of it. My eyes rolled to the back of my head. "Mmm. This is so good. Thank you."

"You're welcome."

"Now that I'm all the way distracted, let me get my thoughts together."

"I'm a lil distracted, too."

I looked up at him and when my eyes met his, they were saying all the things I thought they were. His head lowered, but his eyes were still on mine. I managed to look away and cleared my throat. "So, umm... if you don't mind, I can come over to comb Cassie's hair in the morning and she can ride to school with me. When I was looking over her paperwork, I realized you didn't live far from the school."

He shifted in his seat, then looked back at me. "Sure. That would be cool."

"Also, I would love to spend more time with her outside of school."

His face reddened a little bit, which caught me off-guard and put me on edge. "Are you trying to take my daughter from me, Ms. Washington?"

I lifted my hands in surrender. "No, not at all. I promise. I've just taken a liking to her that I can't explain. She's so sweet and smart and I just want to be a positive influence in her life. As a woman, I mean. I wanted to know if she could spend the day with me Saturday. I wanted to braid her hair and do some girly things with her."

His stare felt like it was piercing my chest. Whereas before, it felt like it was caressing my womanly parts. He didn't trust me because of my forwardness. I got that. He didn't know me. I lowered my gaze to the link on my desk and stared at it for a second longer than I should have. When I looked back up at him, there was a smirk on his lips. "Why don't you eat before it gets cold? I think I can trust a woman that loves food."

I smiled nervously but didn't hesitate to take another bite out of that link. I closed my eyes and didn't look back at Mr. Daniels until I was finished. He had an amused look on his face and his arms were crossed across his chest. "Look. If you can promise me I don't have anything to worry about, I'll allow it."

I smiled, then wiped my mouth. "This link was amazing. It wasn't too greasy, and I think it's the best I've ever eaten. For real."

He laughed and damn. I stared at him, confused as hell. "You make me so comfortable. That shit ain't been done in a long time. The way you killed that link... man, you my kind of woman. Then it's like you can't focus on anything but that."

I rolled my eyes and laughed, too. "So, can I get Cassie tomorrow?"

"That works. I have to work, and I was gonna have to bring her with me. My brother has to go out of town, which was why I had to take off today to pick up Cassie."

"Listen, Mr. Daniels."

"Price. Call me Price."

"Okay. Well, outside of school, call me Kendall."

I smiled at him and he smiled back. My panties were wet, and I almost couldn't control the trembling of my legs. "Price, whatever you need me to do for Cassie, I'm more than able to do it. I'm single and I don't have any children."

"You really love her, huh?"

"I really do."

He glanced at my flowers, then looked back at me as he stood from his seat. "Well, umm... I guess I should go."

He glanced at the flowers once again. I was waiting for him to ask whatever it was that he was thinking. "So, tomorrow, I should bring her to your house, right?"

"Yes. I'll send you my address through text, if that's okay."

I stood from my seat and walked around the desk to stand next to him. He had to be about six-two because I was five-seven and he towered over me. My entire body heated up when he grabbed my hand. "I told you that you could text me anytime."

That statement had an underlying meaning that I couldn't miss. I was uncomfortable, because I wanted this man to throw me on top of this desk and have his way with me. He released my hand and stepped away from me and said, "My bad. You just... you're so sweet. And I appreciate what you're doing for Cassie. She's been so happy since you've been doing her hair. Yours is beautiful, too, by the way."

My face heated up tremendously for the second time today. *Why was I tripping?* This was my student's father. I needed to control my wayward thoughts. "Thank you, Mr. Daniels."

He gave me the side-eye, then said, "Price."

"Right. Price."

He licked his lips again and I knew I had to get him the hell out of here. The kids were about to come back in the next ten minutes anyway. "Ms. Washington, thanks again. I should get to your house about seven. Is that too early?"

"It's early, but Cassie and I can go back to sleep for a little while."

"Okay. Don't forget to send me your address. She'll be happy to know that she doesn't have to go to work with me tomorrow, riding in an eighteen-wheeler all day."

"I would be happy, too, if I were her."

He smiled at me and I couldn't help but close my eyes. He knew what he was doing to me. I opened my eyes to find him staring at me. "Kendall..." He bit his bottom lip, causing my heart to race. "Let me take you and Cassie to dinner Saturday evening when I get off."

He glanced at the flowers for the third time. "If it's okay with whoever sent those flowers."

I glanced back at the flowers, thinking of West. "I'm sin-gle," I said, enunciating the word. "I don't have to ask permission from anyone to go anywhere I please. And let me think on dinner."

He gave me a one-sided smile, then walked to the door. I followed him and when he turned around to say something else, I damn near walked into him. He caught me by the waist. I stared in his eyes and I could have sworn I saw Jesus with his arms outstretched, welcoming me home. *Damn.* He leaned in slightly and I quickly backed away. "I'm so sorry, Mr. Daniels. I'll send my address in a little bit and I'll see you and Cassie in the morning."

I was so un-fucking-professional. If he ever got angry with me and wanted to get me back for something, he could report my behavior and get me fired. While I didn't feel like he would do that, I needed to protect my job. "Yes, ma'am. Enjoy the rest of your day."

He walked out the classroom and I literally had to go to the bathroom to dab my face with a wet paper towel. God himself was gonna have to blow on me to cool me off. Thank God we only had two hours of school left.

CHAPTER 4

P rice

WHEN I LEFT THE SCHOOL, I had to sit in my truck for a hot minute. Kendall Washington had me tripping. She was my daughter's teacher but damn. She was fine as hell and watching her eat that link had me wanting to lick the sauce off her fingers. Her light pink, pointed nails made those fingers even more appealing. All I could think about was how they would feel sliding down the back of my head while I dug her out. I had to mentally check out a few times. If I would've gotten hard, I wouldn't have been able to hide it.

As I sat there, I sent her a text. *I'm sorry if I made you uncomfortable.* I really wasn't sorry, because I could see that she was trying to fight this shit just like I was. I believed we were fighting it for two totally different reasons, though. Somebody was seriously trying to be with her if he'd sent a bouquet like that. It had to set him back at least two-hundred-dollars. I couldn't even think about spending that kind of money on some shit that was gon' die in a couple of days, regardless of how good it made her feel.

What was I thinking? She couldn't be attracted to a man like me. I didn't have a lot of money and I surely couldn't provide anything that she couldn't provide for herself. I started the truck and as I was about to put it in gear, I received a text from her. What it said made my eyebrows raise. *There's no need for an apology. It was a good uncomfortable. There's a mutual attraction between us. But I'm Cassie's teacher.*

I didn't know what she meant by that, but after her admission, I didn't care. I texted her back. *And? What Cassie don't know won't hurt her.*

I didn't expect an immediate response, because I knew the kids were probably back in class. I headed to the apartment and started cooking so Cassie could eat after doing homework, if she had any. It was Friday. I was never the one to help her with homework, so I wasn't used to the routine yet. Once I seasoned the drumsticks and put them in the oven, my phone chimed. Looking at it, I saw it was a text from Ms. Washington. *Cassie's a smart girl. I don't want to give her a false sense of hope.*

False sense of hope? I guess she was saying she would never seriously consider being with somebody like me. She didn't know me. She knew enough, though. I had a daughter that I was struggling to provide for... or at least that was what it looked like. I decided not to respond to her. I continued cooking, but her face never left my thoughts. *Why she had to be so damn fine?*

I set the timer on the oven after putting on a pot of rice and laid on the sofa to watch TV. With as many hours as I'd been working, I found that I spent most of my free time sleeping. So just in case I fell asleep, the oven timer would wake me up. I needed to check the chicken in thirty minutes anyway. Laying there, I couldn't help but think about Kendall. The TV was watching me, because I hadn't seen a thing. To get my mind off her for a moment, I called my brother to see if they'd made it safely. "Hello?"

"What's up, bruh? Y'all made it to Mississippi yet?"

"Yeah. We actually just got to the hospital to see her dad. It's not looking good, man."

"I'm sorry, Karter. Well, go be with your wife and kids, man. I just wanted to make sure y'all had made it there."

"Aight. Talk to you later."

I ended the call and took a deep breath. I felt for Tricia. I knew what it was like to lose parents. If I were to be totally honest with myself, I still wasn't over it. Losing them in that car crash was devastating. It didn't help that I was going through bullshit with Cassie's mama at the time, either. She'd refused to let Cassie come be with me until the funeral. My baby had to be alone grieving the loss of the only grandparents she knew, all alone.

I was still tripping on the fact that Shayla hadn't even tried to call, especially after I'd gone to the attorney general's office and stopped the child support payments. I had a court date next week, that I'd already taken off for. I'd also taken off the weekend after, so I could spend some time with my baby. It helped that I was getting double pay for working Monday, since it was Labor Day. *Shit.* Karter still wouldn't be back, so I'd have to ask Ms. Washington to keep Cassie.

Grabbing my phone, I decided to look her up on Facebook. I almost didn't recognize her with her hair pulled into a bun, similar to the one she'd put in my baby's hair yesterday. Going to her profile, I saw she was thirty-three years old. Damn. She was a whole five years older than me. That was okay, though. Twenty-eight wasn't too terribly young. But then again, it didn't matter. My wallet probably wasn't fat enough for her.

I noticed she wore four rings and the pearls in her ears and around her neck said she liked nice things. Continuing to scroll, I noticed there were mostly pictures of her and two other women, one that looked a lot like her. That was probably her sister. I was surprised to see her page was public since she was a schoolteacher. Going to her pictures, I almost lost my shit. Sitting straight up on the sofa, I enlarged the picture to see her in a bikini. All that ass, just hanging out of those bottoms only heightened my growing erection. Those thick thighs were begging me to get between them.

Just as I was about to get carried away and pull my dick out, the timer on the oven went off. I friend requested her, then sat my phone on the couch to check the chicken. It needed about another twenty minutes, then I'd have to leave to go get Cassie. I sat back on the sofa and continued to scroll Facebook. I then received a text. *You don't give up easily, do you?*

I slowly shook my head. She didn't want me to give up, but I knew leaving her on read would irritate her. While I almost did that shit anyway, I went ahead and responded. *Nope.*

I smiled as I sent it, then put my feet up on the coffee table. She was gonna give in to what she was feeling, even if it was just a kiss. I could see her staring at my lips when I licked them. I had no problem showing her how much I wanted her. However, I knew since she was at work, it was hard for her to be as open. The true test would be tomorrow morning. I couldn't wait to see her first thing in the morning. Seeing her without the makeup would be the true test. It wasn't like she wore a lot of it, but I wanted to see her fresh out the bed.

If she could hold my attention, there was no way I would allow her to continue this game. She would either talk to me and acknowledge what she was feeling, or our relationship would have to be strictly professional. As hard as that would be, I wouldn't be able to go there with her. My phone chimed letting me know she'd sent another message. Expecting to see her name, I quickly grabbed my phone to see a text from my brother. *He passed away. It was like he was waiting on Tricia to get here.*

My shoulders slumped as I thought about how I knew she had to be feeling. Because her dad lived in Jackson, Mississippi, they only visited twice a year; during the summer and for New Years. They always spent Christmas with me... or rather I spent it with them. I hadn't had anyone in my life since I stopped fucking with Shayla when Cassie was two years old. I'd fucked around but not had a real girlfriend. So, since our parents had been killed, we'd made a vow to always stick together and look out for each other.

I sent a message back. *I'm so sorry. Tell Tricia that I'm praying for y'all. You need anything?*

Him: *No, but thanks. The only issue is that we won't be coming back until Thursday. So, that'll leave you without transportation for Cassie. Tricia has a friend that has a daughter that goes there, and I could ask her to get Cassie.*

Me: *Don't worry about Cassie. I've got it handled. Just focus on your family right now. I love y'all.*

Him: *Love you, too, bruh. I'll call you later tonight.*

The timer went off once again, so I took the chicken from the oven, then prepared to head out. My phone chimed again, and that was Ms. Washington. *I admire persistence.*

She was playing games already. I slowly shook my head and headed to the school to get in the pickup line. That line could get long as shit and I wasn't trying to be in it all day. Hopefully, Kendall didn't have duty. I couldn't look at her without my dick getting excited. Since she didn't know what she wanted yet, I couldn't show her all I had to offer. I thought I would try to woo her at first, but fuck that. We'd be around one another concerning Cassie. Being myself was never a problem.

She had options, so I'd sit back and wait. I was always patient. Back when I was eighteen, I'd let Shayla know I was interested, then I chilled out until she came to me. She was supposedly talking to some nigga back then that she thought was gonna give her the world. Then when he went ghost on her, she looked me up. I should've left her ass right where she was, but then I wouldn't have Cassie. That lil girl was the best thing that ever happened to me.

When I found out Shayla was pregnant, I enrolled in truck driving school at LIT and dropped the classes I was taking at the university. She was pissed, because she didn't wanna be with no truck driver. She stopped complaining once the checks started coming in, though. The school was only for six weeks, but it gave you the same experience as someone that had been driving for two years. I was making more money than teachers were making. That's how I knew things wouldn't be tight always, but I was working for something. I was trying to make sure me and Cassie could live comfortably within the next couple of years. It took some sacrifice, but so far, I had thirty grand saved up, including the ten grand I had left from my parents insurance policy. Once it got to forty grand, I would start looking for a house.

The bell was finally ringing, and I was ready to start the weekend. I didn't know why, since I would be working tomorrow and Monday. The only day I would have with Cassie was Sunday. I normally went to church, but since Cassie had been with me, I hadn't gone. I didn't want to bring her with her hair everywhere. Since Ms. Washington was going to braid it tomorrow, we'd be sure to go this Sunday.

The line began moving, so I put the truck in gear and eased up as kids got tossed into their rides. I couldn't be a teacher, dealing with bad ass kids all day. As I approached the awning where the kids were, I got a text. *Look up.*

When I did, I saw Kendall walking across the parking lot with her flowers in her hand. But those thick ass legs peeping through the slits in her dress were calling me. She winked at me as a car honked. I had a gap between me and the car in front of me; a nice sized gap. As I eased up, I looked over at Kendall again and she winked at me as she got in her BMW. Man, she was gon' make me lose my shit and she didn't even wanna try to be with me. It was cool, though. I wasn't about to play games with her.

She had better not do that flirting shit face to face or I was gonna give her what she was asking for. I'd snatch her ass up so fast, it would leave her dizzy. Then I'd lay my lips on them soft looking lips of hers and have her eating out the palm of my hand. She didn't know who she was fucking with, but I was more than willing to show her. And I wouldn't have a problem doing that shit in front of Cassie. I didn't mind showing love to anybody in front of my daughter. But I never wanted her to see or hear me arguing with anybody.

My last female friend almost made me snatch her up in front of Cassie. Once I'd brought Cassie home, I nearly choked her ass. I told her if she ever acted a fool like that again in front of my daughter, I'd hurt her ass. She took heed and stopped hanging around me. I was glad she did, because the last thing I wanted to do was put my hands on a woman. She had started pushing all my buttons.

I drove up to the pick-up line and saw my baby girl standing there with a huge grin on her face. Her hair was beautiful, and I was grateful for Ms. Washington. When she got in, she kissed my cheek, then buckled up. "How was your day, baby?

"It was good! Ms. Washington said I'm going to her house tomorrow! I can't wait! We are going to have so much fun. She said she was going to braid my hair, too."

She continued to ramble on and on and I couldn't help but smile. She was never that excited about anything. I knew she missed her mama, but I hoped she wasn't thinking Ms. Washington was there to take her place.

CHAPTER 5

K endall

"I WAS SO EXCITED. I couldn't help but get here early."

I smiled at West as he stood on my doorstep. He wasn't supposed to pick me up until six-thirty, but here he was... at my house at five-thirty. I didn't know him like that, but I guess if I was going to be in a car alone with him, a house would be about the same. "Umm... okay. Come in."

He walked in the house, carrying another bouquet of flowers. I smiled politely and accepted them, then sat them next to the other bouquet. "Have a seat. As you can see, I'm not quite ready. I wasn't expecting you for another hour. Would you like something to drink while you wait?"

"Sure. A bottle of water will be fine. I'm sorry if I made you feel uncomfortable. That wasn't my intent."

I smiled at him, then handed him the water I'd retrieved from the fridge. "It's okay. I should be done in about forty minutes."

I walked back to my room, looking over my shoulder every step of the way. When I got to my room, I locked the door, then went to the bathroom to finish applying my makeup. I briefly thought about Price and Cassie and what they were probably doing. Picking up my phone, I sent him my address. I'd forgotten to earlier, because I was so damned heated. Price was so fine, but I couldn't pursue anything with him while Cassie was in my class. There was no rule that said I couldn't, but it looked so unprofessional.

After I applied my eye shadow, my phone chimed with a message from him. *I thought you'd changed your mind. See you tomorrow, beautiful.*

He was causing my body to start a war with my good sense. West was in my living room and he looked fine as ever. He'd worn some gray slacks and a navy-blue shirt. His lean frame, neatly trimmed beard, and manicured nails screamed metrosexual and I was cool with that as long as he didn't try to outshine me. I didn't think he would, because there was something street about him. He had diamond studs in his ears, three neck tattoos, and I was pretty sure there were more tattoos underneath his clothes. He was just so intriguing. The fact that he'd gotten here an hour early, though, made me uneasy.

After applying my makeup, I glanced at my phone, tempted to message Price back, but I restrained myself. Walking into my room, I took out my yellow pants, along with the matching top. It went over one shoulder, leaving the other exposed and showed a little of my stomach. I'd brought my hair up into a tight chignon at the top of my head. After accenting my outfit with gold jewelry and nude, three-inch heels, I adjusted the yellow belt on my pants and grabbed my nude clutch.

When I walked into the living room, he was sitting on the sofa playing on his phone. I'd managed to be ready in thirty minutes. West looked up at me and immediately stood from his seat. "Damn, you're beautiful."

"Thank you, West. I'm sorry I didn't tell you earlier, but you look very nice as well."

"Thank you."

"Let me put these flowers in water and I'll be ready."

"Okay. Let me help you. Sorry I didn't get a bouquet like earlier, so you would have a vase."

"It's okay."

He was nervous as hell. So nervous until he was overdoing it. I stood closer to him and I could hear his breathing quicken. Looking up at him, I grabbed his hand. "West. Cool out."

He smiled at me, then lifted my hand to those tinted lips. He kissed the top of it. "I just wanna impress you. That's all."

"Don't worry. Just be yourself."

He smiled at me as I turned on the faucet water to fill an empty vase. After we'd arranged the roses in it, we washed our hands and headed for the door. Once I locked up, West held his arm out for me to grab ahold of, then led me to his SUV. He opened my door and assisted me with getting inside, then closed it. I sat there feeling like Queen Bee. I lifted my phone and took a quick selfie to send to my sister and Peyton.

West joined me inside, then said, "I hope you like Italian food. Is Carrabba's okay?"

"Yeah. That's fine. I've only been there once, but I'd been meaning to go back. So, it's perfect."

West smiled, then grabbed my hand and held it all the way there. The awkwardness was gone, and he seemed to be more at ease. After parking, he turned to me and said, "They usually get pretty crowded, so I guess it's a good thing that we're a little early."

I smiled at him as he walked around to open my door. Again, he bent his arm for me to grab ahold of, then led me to the entrance. When he opened the door for me, I walked through, then waited for him to join me. He told the hostess of the reservation, then she led us to a booth. Once seated, he stared at me for a moment, then said, "I'm so glad I met you Wednesday night."

"I'm glad, too, especially since I didn't want to go on a school night."

He chuckled. "It was destined for us to meet. So how do you plan to spend your weekend?"

"Well, one of my students is coming over tomorrow and I plan to braid her hair and take her shopping."

"Wow. That's great that you're that involved. You remind me of the teachers I had growing up. They always went above and beyond to make sure their students were good."

"Yes. As a little girl, I always said I wanted to be a teacher like Mrs. Johns. She was my third-grade teacher that always took extra time with us."

"That's great. Well, on Sunday, would you like to go to brunch?"

"Hmm. Sure. Who serves brunch besides Suga's?"

"I don't know. I was gonna take you to Suga's."

He smiled brightly as the waitress came to the table to take our drink orders. Maybe tonight wouldn't be so bad. Things seemed to be going well. And the evening was flowing smoothly. Nothing seemed forced and I was comfortable, unlike earlier.

After dinner, we headed to the movie theater, but the movie West wanted to take me to see was sold out. It was the last showing for the night. He looked angry and somewhat embarrassed. "West, it's cool. Maybe we can come another time, like Sunday after brunch."

"Yeah."

I noticed he had calmed down a bit as we walked back to his vehicle. Once we'd gotten in, he asked, "So, what do you want to do now?"

"We can watch a movie at my place, if that's cool with you."

"As long as I'm spending time with you, it's cool with me."

I smiled at him as he lifted my hand and kissed it. He was so romantic, but I could see there was something dark about him. That flicker of anger when he found out the movie was sold out put me on guard for a moment. But all seemed good now and I couldn't wait to spend more time with him.

~

WHEN THE DOORBELL RANG, I hopped out of bed. *Shit!* I'd over-slept. Running to the bathroom, I quickly gargled just to make sure my breath didn't stink, then made my way to the door. When I got to it, I could see Cassie hopping around excitedly while Price laughed at her. That made me smile. As I unlocked the door, she stopped hopping and just stared straight ahead. Once I opened it, my eyes met Price's. His eyes scanned from my head wrap down to my white toenails. "Good morning, beautiful," I said to Cassie.

"Good morning, Ms. Washington!"

I smiled at her excited eyes, then invited them in. "Good morning, Mr. Daniels."

"Good morning, Ms. Washington. You have a nice home."

"Thank you."

He remained at the door as Cassie wondered around. His eyes were on me and my body was heating up like someone had put a blow torch on me. I'd just had an amazing night with West, but the things Price made my body feel should have been illegal. While I felt amazing with West, he didn't ignite the fire that Price had blazing every time he looked at me. But for whatever reason, my mind felt like that fire was gonna burn me, so I wanted to stay safe. West seemed safe. "Has Cassie eaten yet?"

"Yeah. She had eggs, biscuits, and bacon. I cook for her every morning."

His eyes once again scanned my body, so I gave him something to see. Under my robe, I wore some tight shorts that stopped at mid-thigh and a tank top. Allowing my robe to fall open, I let a smirk play on my lips. He licked his lips, then his eyes met mine. "You like to play games, huh?"

"I've been known to be a tease."

He looked up to see Cassie in the kitchen, looking around, then looked back at me. "Being a tease gon' get you fucked."

His voice was low and steady, and his gaze seemed to be penetrating my kitty with the way it gushed at his words. My lips parted and I slowly tied my robe. There were no smiles, smirks, or anything to indicate he was playing. Glancing down, I saw movement in his pants. "Ms. Washington?"

Tearing my gaze away from his, I looked at Cassie in the kitchen. She was standing at the island looking at all the hair products I'd purchased and bundles of hair. "Yes, sweetheart?"

"This is a lot of hair."

I chuckled. "Yeah, it is. I'm doing my hair, too."

She smiled at me and I turned my attention back to Price. His eyes were still on me. "So, what time will you get off?"

"Six. Are you letting me take you to dinner with me and Cassie?"

"I'm sorry, but no. I can't. I have to braid my hair."

"Aight. Well, I gotta go." He looked over at his daughter. "Cassie, I'm about to leave."

She ran to him and hugged him tightly around his waist. Watching them love on each other was a little overwhelming and made me wish I had a kid. He bent over slightly and kissed her head. She went back to the kitchen to finish looking through the things I'd bought. Price looked at me again. "Have a good day at work."

He took out his wallet and tried to give me some money. "Cassie said y'all might go shopping. I got paid yesterday and I'd promised to take her to get some clothes she liked. But since y'all are going..."

He shrugged his shoulders. I looked down to see two-hundred-dollars in his hand. I extended my hand to take it from him and as I did, he grabbed my hand. My eyes closed involuntarily but opened when I heard his voice. "I know you feel that, but I'm gon' let'chu do you until you can't no more. It's only a matter of time before you gon' see that you belong to me."

Once again, my lips parted, but no sound left my mouth. His eyes scanned me once again, then he turned to leave as I watched him. After closing the door, I leaned against it for a second. This man... *what was he doing to me?* Turning to Cassie, I found her looking at me with a smile on her face. "Well, you ready to get started on your hair?"

"Yes, ma'am!"

I giggled. "Well, let me get cleaned up and I'll be right back to get started."

"Okay!"

I turned the big screen TV on to the Disney channel and watched her eyes light up, then headed to my room. I yelled back, "If you need anything, just come knock on my door. It's the last one down the hallway."

"Yes ma'am."

She was such a sweet girl and I couldn't wait to spend time with her. However, her dad was gonna be the death of me.

CHAPTER 6

P rice

I'D TEXTED Ms. Washington several times already to check on my baby. Cassie was always either with me or my brother. I really didn't know Ms. Washington like that, but if I wanted help, I had to trust her. That ass was on hush though while I was right in front of her. If she wasn't gon' give me a chance, then she wasn't gon' tease me either. Although I knew her body wanted to see what I could dish out, her analytical mind was holding her back. She was an over-thinker. I knew if there ever came a time that I could just snatch her up, she wouldn't fight me, because she wouldn't be able to. When she let her robe open, I could see that her nipples were hard as hell. It was plain to see that I turned her on.

I had another hour before I would get back to the yard, so I called to check on Cassie. As the phone rang, I couldn't help but think about how perfect a relationship with Kendall would be. She already loved my baby and that was a huge positive. Finding a woman that loved a child that wasn't related to her as much as she already loved Cassie was rare. Kendall answered on the third ring. "Hello, Mr. Daniels. We're at Target, balling out of control."

I could hear Cassie laughing in the background. There was no way they could ball out of control with only two-hundred-dollars. "Sounds like y'all having fun. Don't break the bank, though."

Shit, I couldn't afford to give her anything more, not without sacrificing my lunches and my Friday scratch off tickets. That was my guilty pleasure. I'd won pretty big a couple of times, but most of my wins had been minor; just winning back the money I'd spent in a month's time. Before Kendall could respond, I heard another female talking and my baby girl responding to her. "Don't worry, Mr. Daniels. I got this covered. You just concentrate on whatever you're doing."

I chuckled. "Aight. What my baby hair look like? Send me a picture."

"Nope. You'll see it when you get off. She wants you to be surprised."

"It looks that good, huh?"

"Well, not to toot my own horn, but toot toot."

I laughed again. She was more relaxed, and I knew that was because I wasn't in her face. I could see how sexually tense she was at her house. She was lucky Cassie was always around me or she would have gotten just what she was searching for. "Aight. Well, I'll see y'all right at six. They moved a little faster today, so I should get home at five. After I shower, I'll be there. You know, it's okay to change your mind."

"Thanks for the invite, but I really have to do my hair tonight. My sister came to meet me so she can help. It takes a long time to braid all of this hair."

"Aight. Tell my baby I'll see her in a lil bit."

"Okay," she said softly.

She confused the hell out of me. Her mannerisms were saying that she wanted me, but her mouth was saying that it wasn't a good idea. It seemed that she was as confused as she was making me. I ended the call and drove down IH-10 east, my mind far away from what my eyes were looking at. It was on how I felt being so close to her. My dick was ready to tear something up, and I believed she noticed. He was uncontrollable where she was concerned. Lately, I'd been a professional at keeping him in check, but her ass was making me look like an amateur.

Because of the size of my shit, if I got hard with my work pants on, he would undeniably steal the show. That had only happened once and the guard in the shack where I waited to be loaded eyes had gotten wide as hell. I was flirting with her and she was flirting back as I was getting my paperwork. She was sexy as hell. And my dick couldn't help but express to her just how sexy she was. Needless to say, after that day we fucked several times until her and her man got back together. Even after that, she'd called me a few times. I didn't fuck with people's relationships, though. If she wanted to keep fucking me, she should have stayed single.

When I finally got back to the yard and parked, I did my paperwork and made a bee line to my place. It was the same way every time I got off. I wanted to get to Cassie as soon as possible. Since I didn't get to spend a lot of time with her, all my free time was dedicated to her and I didn't want to waste a minute of that. Now, if she chose to get on her tablet or watch TV without me, then that was okay. But I wanted her to see that she was my world and that, regardless of her mom's actions, I loved her with my whole heart. She was wanted more than anything else.

I believed that was why she took to Ms. Washington so easily. She was missing her mom and the comfort of a woman that looked like her. Tricia was cool, but because she was white, I believed it was harder for Cassie to bond with her in that way. She and Ms. Washington had a lot in common. Although Cassie was a lighter complexion, Ms. Washington was a black woman that could relate to her. She had hair like her and spoke the same way she did. I believed Cassie admired her sense of style, too. That was why she was so excited about going shopping with her.

After taking my shower, I got dressed in some distressed jeans, my white Forces, and a white shirt, then sprayed some Nautica cologne on my shirt. Women seemed to love that fragrance on me, and I wanted to have Kendall even more sexually charged than she was this morning. She said her sister would be there, so she would probably try to contain herself. After brushing my brown waves in my faded haircut and brushing my beard, I grabbed my keys and headed out.

I planned to take my baby to Cheddar's. She absolutely loved their spinach dip and the grilled cheese. To say she started school three days late, she jumped right in and didn't lag behind. She'd already gotten a progress report and she had straight A's, nothing under a ninety-five. I already knew she was smart, but with all that was going on, I was praying that it didn't affect her negatively. While she was sad at times, she continued to do well in school and when I asked how she was feeling, she told me the truth. Once we'd talk through her issues, dealing with her mother's abandonment, she seemed to perk up.

Once I got to Kendall's house, I noticed two other cars in the driveway. I knew that one was her sister, but I wasn't sure who the other car was for. I supposed I'd find out in a minute. Exiting my truck, I walked to the front door and before I could ring the doorbell, a woman opened the door with a huge smile on her face. "Hi! You must be Cassie's dad."

"Yes, ma'am, I am."

"Come on in. I'm Kendall's best friend Peyton, but everybody calls me P."

I shook her outstretched hand after she closed the door. "Nice to meet you."

"I'm actually standing here to make the introduction."

I frowned slightly, because I didn't have a clue of what she was talking about. Before I could question what she was talking about, she continued, "Introducing, the eight-year-old model, taking the fashion world by storm, Miss Cassie Lanay Daniels!"

I chuckled as Cassie came walking down the hallway. My eyes widened at how gorgeous my baby was. They'd made her face up and she wore a dress that stopped at her knees along with some wedge heels. Her braids were gorgeous and had clear beads on the ends. Watching her try to walk like a model was humorous and I did my best not to laugh. However, I couldn't stop the big ass smile that was on my face. She twirled, then remained still for a moment. P started clapping, so I joined her applauding my little girl.

Cassie smiled brightly, then ran to me. "Daddy, what do you think?" she asked excitedly.

"I think you are the most beautiful little girl in the world. And I'm so glad you're mine."

She hugged me as I noticed Kendall coming down the hallway with another woman I took to be her sister. I then realized P and this other lady were the women I'd seen in Kendall's Facebook pictures. Cassie ran to her and exclaimed, "He loved it!"

I smiled at Kendall as she walked toward me with bags of clothes. I noticed her sister had bags as well. "Hi, Mr. Daniels. I'm Alana, Ms. Washington's sister."

"Nice to meet you," I said while shaking her hand.

I could see the looks she and P were giving Kendall. There was some type of communication going on that I wasn't privy to, but I was almost sure it had something to do with me. Kendall looked up at me. "Seeing her this happy is so rewarding. Thank you so much."

Alana sat the bags on the sofa, then took the bags from Kendall and sat them there as well. "You're welcome, Mr. Daniels," she said somewhat softly.

She cleared her throat and Alana and P giggled. I gathered they'd been talking about me. "So, as far as her hair is concerned, at night, just pull it into a ponytail and tie a head scarf on it. I bought one at the beauty supply store, along with a silk cap to put on it to cover the ponytail. Don't worry about doing anything else to her hair until maybe Tuesday morning. Just put a little oil on her scalp. Everything you need is in these bags. Of course, you could always call or text me if you need anything."

My eyes never left hers as she spoke. The way she stared at me; I knew she was feeling a way. P cleared her throat and Kendall looked away. "Thanks again, Ms. Washington."

I looked over at Cassie and she was in her own world, playing on her tablet, occasionally looking at the beads hanging in her face. I grabbed Kendall's hand and pulled her to me, hugging her. The way her body molded into mine made me wanna just swoop her up and carry her to the bedroom. I was so close to kissing her cheek before letting go. "You didn't have to do any of the things you did today, or any of what you will most likely continue to do. Cassie and I are so blessed to have you in our lives."

She stared up in my eyes. "I love Cassie. There's nothing I wouldn't do for her."

I licked my lips as she spoke, watching her lips form words was turning me on. Shifting my gaze to Cassie, I asked, "Well, you ready for dinner, baby girl?"

"Okay. Where are we going?"

"Your favorite place."

"Cheddar's?" she asked excitedly.

I smiled at her. "Yep."

"Today has been amazing!"

I couldn't help but chuckle. As Kendall slid her hand from mine, I didn't even realize I was holding it. *Damn.* It just felt so natural. "My bad," I said softly.

She shook her head, indicating that it wasn't a problem, I assumed. Walking over to her sofa, I grabbed the bags and she grabbed some as well. Cassie had a couple of bags in her hands. "Nice meeting you, ladies," I said, realizing they'd gone to the kitchen.

I was so damn wrapped up in Kendall, I hadn't seen them walk away. We walked through the front door to my truck. Thankfully, I had a backseat, because like Kendall had said earlier, they had balled out of control. Once I'd gotten all the bags inside and Cassie had gotten in and buckled up, I turned to Kendall. Damn, she was so beautiful. Grabbing her hand, I brought it to my lips and kissed it. "Thank you again. I owe you. So, whenever you wanna go to dinner, let me know."

She smiled softly but didn't respond verbally. I turned to get in my truck as she said, "Thank you for trusting me with Cassie. We had an amazing time. Maybe she can join me and P on Monday for barbeque at my parents' house."

"That would be cool. I have to work Monday, so I was gonna ask you to watch her and it slipped my mind."

I scanned her beautiful walnut complexion from head to toe and I could have sworn that I saw her tremble. "Okay, well, I'll see y'all Monday morning."

I nodded, then got in my truck before I fucked around and kissed those beautiful pink lips. When I closed the door, Cassie asked, "You like Ms. Washington, huh Daddy?"

"What if I said yeah?"

"Then I'd say that I think she likes you, too."

She was paying closer attention than what I thought, but it didn't seem to bother her. Instead of entertaining the conversation, I turned up the music and backed out the driveway as her glossed lips spread into a smile.

CHAPTER 7

K endall

"Bitch! You wanna pick your tongue up off the floor? I ain't never seen you tripping over a man like that!"

"Shut up, Alana."

"Kendall, she's right, girl. What's up? I mean, Mr. Daniels is fine as hell, but I thought things went well with West last night?"

"Honestly, it's like a fire ignites within me whenever I see Price and I can't control the shit."

"Price? Oh, that must be his first name. Damn, sis. Yo' ass got it bad."

Alana and P both laughed loudly, like some damn hyenas. I rolled my eyes as I flopped on the sofa. My mind had been on Price all day, even while I was talking to West. I pulled my bun loose so I could wash my hair and briefly thought about Price grabbing a handful of it while he pounded me from behind. The soft moan that left my lips brought me out of the trance I was in. Alana and P were staring at me like I was crazy. *Maybe I was.*

I could not have a relationship with my student's father. *What's stopping you from fucking him?* My thoughts were about to drive me insane! "I can't pursue anything with him, though."

"Why not?"

"He's my student's father."

"And? What the fuck that got to do with anything?" Alana asked loudly.

"Because if things don't work out, it would be awkward as hell having his daughter in my class and having to possibly deal with him as a parent and scorned lover."

"Well damn, sis. Why would he have to be scorned?"

I took a deep breath. "Can you be serious for once, Alana?"

"So, this is serious?"

I closed my eyes. It seemed to be getting serious. My body wanted him so badly, it was about to take action without me. This shit was unexplainable. After opening my eyes, I could see them looking at me seriously, waiting on an answer as my phone rang. When I saw Price's number, I took in air and slowly released it, then answered. "Hello?"

"Hi, Ms. Washington! I just wanted to say thank you again. I had so much fun! You wanna come to church with us tomorrow? You'll like our church," Cassie rambled.

Before I could answer, she whispered, "Plus, my dad likes you, and I think you like him, too."

That was the very thing I was trying to avoid. I didn't want to get her hopes up, thinking that her dad and I would be together. She was vulnerable and sensitive right now, looking for someone to replace her mother. "I'm sorry, sweetheart. I can't go. I already have plans for tomorrow."

"Oh."

Hearing her disappointment made me wanna cancel my plans with West, but I couldn't do that to him. He was a nice guy that deserved a chance. *West was safe.* "Well, I just wanted to say thank you again."

"You're welcome, baby."

She ended the call and my spirit felt crushed. Cassie sounded so sad and it seemed I was attached to her already. Before I could let Alana and Peyton in on what had just happened, my phone rang again. It was West. *Shit. I couldn't answer his call right now.* I silenced the ringer and went to the bathroom to wash my hair, Alana and P hot on my trail. "Doll, you okay?"

Just P calling me doll had me all sensitive and shit. She only called me that when she knew I was feeling sensitive and fragile like a porcelain doll. "I'm okay. I just hated hearing the disappointment in Cassie's voice when she asked if I could go to church with them tomorrow. And she peeped game. She knows we're feeling each other."

"Well, it didn't seem like y'all were trying to hide the shit, Kendall."

"Lana, I couldn't hide the shit if I tried. Real shit."

"Damn. Why don't you just let go? You can't think about what you'll do if it *won't* work, if you want the shit *to* work. That's like getting married and planning for the divorce."

I exhaled loudly as I got a towel from the cabinet, then took off my shirt. "I don't wanna talk about the shit no more."

And that was the end of that. They knew once I said I didn't want to talk about something anymore, getting me to continue anyway would be like pulling a stripper from the pole with hundred-dollar bills flying in the air.

~

"Ma'am, I called ahead. There's no excuse for us having to wait more than a few minutes. We've been sitting here for twenty minutes."

"I apologize, sir. We weren't prepared for the charter bus that stopped in. We will have a table ready for you as soon as possible."

West grabbed my hand tightly as he turned and pulled me with him to wait. He was angry, because not only had we been waiting a while, but there was nowhere to sit as we waited. My feet were starting to hurt, so I turned to him. "West, if you don't want to wait, we can go somewhere else."

"It's not about having to wait. It's about them disregarding my reservation. That pisses me off," he said a little too loudly.

I was somewhat embarrassed, and I didn't know what the fuck to do other than to slip my shoes off. It was like he was on a rampage about the shit and for me, it wasn't that serious. He walked over to the hostess and said loudly, "I need to speak to your manager."

"Yes, sir."

I closed my eyes, wondering why this nigga was clowning. It was only making me wish I would have canceled on his ass and went to church with Cassie and Price. *Price.* His face appeared in my mind and a small smile came to my lips as I smoothed out my peach colored pants. His words from the other day came to mind. *...You belong to me.* That shit had me so turned on and just thinking about it had my body heating up.

My temperature quickly plummeted when I heard West say, "This is unacceptable. You punish the ones with plans for spur of the moment customers. How is that logical? We've been waiting for thirty minutes now."

"Sir, we're doing everything we can to move people in and out as quickly as possible. We are so sorry for the inconvenience."

"Don't worry. We won't be back."

One of my brows lifted as people stared at me, since I was with him. I rolled my eyes and was about to go stand outside until the manager stated, "We just got a table cleaned for you. Please follow me this way."

He gestured for me to join him and if I wasn't hungry as hell, I would have cursed his ass out. This was such an embarrassing ordeal. I was just ready to go home. Once we sat, the manager stated that we would receive three courses on the house for the inconvenience. I knew I still had a frown on my face, though. "You okay, Kendall? I'm so upset about this. I can see that you're upset, too."

"I'm not upset about having to wait. I'm upset about the spectacle you put on. I'm so embarrassed, West."

His eyebrows lifted as if he was surprised. "I apologize. I just don't like for people to feel like they can walk over me. Embarrassing you was never my intent."

He reached across the table and held his palms up for me to place my hands in his. Hesitantly, I did so. The remorse in his eyes was evident. "I'm so sorry. Really."

"It's cool, West. Let's just try to have a better outing."

He nodded as the waitress came to the table and took our drink and appetizer orders. Once the waitress left, he looked back at me. "So, how was your day yesterday with your student?"

"It was fun. She's such a sweetheart."

"Her mom must be grateful to have someone like you in her life."

"She actually lives with her dad."

"Oh okay. That explains a lot. I couldn't imagine trying to comb a little girl's hair."

I only nodded. None of the particulars were his business. I dug into my salad and it was so delicious. It was full of fresh fruit and pecans. As I ate, I could see West glancing at me. He looked a little nervous. He was probably thinking I was still angry. I wasn't quite angry, but I was definitely irritated. Positive attention was always cool with me, but negative attention, especially when I wasn't the one drawing it, always irritated me and sometimes pissed me off. Had that little debacle gone on any longer, I would have walked out on his ass.

The rest of our time at Suga's had gone well and we were in my driveway. West was acting like he wanted to turn his engine off. "West, I'm not staying home. I'm going to my parents' house to help my mama cook for tomorrow."

"Oh. My bad. I was gonna ask to spend time with you tomorrow."

"I'll also have Cassie tomorrow. Her dad has to work."

He frowned slightly. "Are you sure he isn't using you? Or maybe trying to get next to you?"

I frowned back. He was stepping on all my toes today. This was only our second date and I was ready to curse his ass out. "I like having her around. So, it's a win-win, regardless of his motives. I know their underlying situation and conditions, but that isn't my business to share."

He held his hands in the air. "I didn't mean anything by my question, Kendall. I just didn't want to see you get used. You're obviously still on edge about what happened at Suga's. I'm sorry."

I exhaled loudly. "Okay, West. I'll talk to you later."

As I was about to exit, he grabbed my hand. "You know I would never let you open a door. Please let me do that."

I nodded. When he got out, I closed my eyes and tried to calm my nerves. I hated lying but I didn't feel like being bothered with him anymore. My mama was cooking tomorrow, not today. He opened my door and I got out of his SUV. He grabbed my hand to assist me, then walked me to the door. Once we got there, he stepped closer to me. Although he'd irritated me, that didn't stop him from being a sexy man, and his remorseful face was causing me to melt. Then he poked out his lip and I couldn't help but smile. Pulling me closer to him, he kissed my forehead, then lifted my head by my chin and softly kissed my lips.

I felt nothing.

"See you later, beautiful."

I smiled at him, then turned to unlock my door as he walked away. My body hadn't even heated up. That made me want Price even more, but then I thought that maybe because we didn't have a great date it killed that vibe, too. Once inside, I went to my room and fell in my bed as my phone chimed. I grabbed my clutch and took my phone from it to see a text from Price. I opened it to see a selfie of Cassie. Underneath the picture, she'd typed out, *Hi, Ms. Washington!*

I smiled as I noticed Price had put one of her bows that I'd bought in her braids. Another picture came through and she was wearing one of the dresses we'd bought, also. I responded with heart emojis, then rolled over to my back, staring at the ceiling. The thought of calling them crossed my mind, but I fought against it and decided to walk on my treadmill instead and just chill out. Giving Price a chance was plaguing my thoughts, but I knew that I needed to give it way more thought.

CHAPTER 8

P rice

"Your load has been canceled for tomorrow. So, see you back on Tuesday."

"Aight."

Well, there was that. I didn't have to work tomorrow. I was looking forward to that double pay. Cassie and I had just left Golden Corral. We didn't really have anything planned since I thought I'd have to work tomorrow. I knew I would need to call Kendall back to let her know. Cassie had sent her a couple of text messages after we left church, so I wondered if she was home. She said she had plans, but with as quick as she answered Cassie's text messages, I wondered if they fell through.

After getting home and getting out of our church clothes, I told Cassie that I would take her to the park. She was so excited. "Daddy, can I call Ms. Washington to see if she wants to go?"

"Text her first to see if she's busy, baby."

I watched her excitedly text her, then wait for a response. My phone started to ring, and Cassie's face lit up. "Hi, Ms. Washington!"

Hmm. That was interesting. As I sat pondering about her plans and what she could've had to do, Cassie held the phone out to me. "Ms. Washington wants to talk to you," she said with a smile on her face and wiggling her eyebrows.

I couldn't help but laugh. "Cut it out."

Cassie laughed as well. I took the phone from her. "Hello?"

"Hi, Price," Kendall said softly.

She sounded like either she'd just woken up or she was depressed about something. "Hey, Ms. Washington."

"What park are y'all going to?"

"The one downtown by the Event Center. I don't remember the name of it. You okay?"

"I just woke up from a nap. Give me a few minutes and I'll head that way."

"Aight. See you when you get there."

When I ended the call, Cassie jumped on me. "She's coming! Daddy, make sure you shoot your shot."

"What'chu say to me?"

I laughed so hard. Ain't nobody but Shayla was talking like that around my baby. What the hell an eight-year-old know about shooting a shot? "Daddy, you gotta shoot your shot. You gotta take a chance. I know she likes you, too, even though she won't say."

"What'chu mean she won't say?"

"I told her that I knew she liked you, too, but she didn't respond. If she didn't like you, she would have said no."

"Man, chill out. You too grown, girl." I watched her drop her head, until I said, "But I'm gon' shoot my shot while you playing."

Her head popped up and she had a huge smile on her face. I decided to talk to her like a grown up since she seemed to understand more than what I gave her credit for. I patted the couch for her to come sit next to me. "This isn't as easy as you may think it is. Ms. Washington has to factor in that she's your teacher. If she gives me a chance and for some reason things don't work out, it'll be kind of awkward for the both of us. Neither of us want to hurt you either. So, if she gives us a chance, it won't be serious until we really get to know each other. Okay?"

"I understand, Daddy. Mama had boyfriends all the time. This past summer, she said she was living a hot girl summer. What does that mean?"

I could feel my face heating up, so I knew it had to be red. I wanted to bitch slap Shayla and I didn't even know where the fuck she was. "Don't worry, baby. It ain't nothing you need to know about."

"You think Mama gon' come back for me?"

"I hope not. I won't be able to let'chu go, now. You want her to come back and get you?"

She shrugged her shoulders. "I don't know, but I like it here."

She missed her mama. I knew things weren't great here in the beginning, but they were getting better. If I had to, I'd pay Kendall to keep Cassie looking fly. The happiness I see in her now is addicting. I couldn't let her go back to the way she was before Kendall got involved in our lives. "Well, you ready to go?"

"Yes, sir."

We stood from the couch and headed out the door. Cassie's happiness was on my mind. I knew she missed her mama, but I was hoping that she was getting past her not being here. I guess I underestimated just how close they were. "Can we go to Dairy Queen when we leave the park?"

"We'll get ice cream from somewhere, baby. Would you prefer Dairy Queen? Baskin Robbins has great ice cream."

"I like Dairy Queen, Daddy."

"Okay, princess."

I continued driving until we got to the park. The minute we safely crossed the street, Cassie took off for the swings. As I sat at a picnic table and watched her, someone said, "So, this is what y'all do on Sundays?"

I looked up to see Kendall. Standing from my seat, I grabbed her hand to assist her. "You look beautiful, and your braids are beautiful, too. They're just like Cassie's. She'll be excited about that."

I was still holding her hand and it was intentional this time. She looked in my eyes and she looked a little tired or troubled. I couldn't make out what it was. Tilting my head to the side, I asked, "You okay?"

"Yeah. My nap was only twenty minutes. It seems I needed a little more."

She chuckled, then slid her hand from mine. "I'm gonna go play for a little while. You wanna come?"

She bit her bottom lip. "That sounds like a loaded question, but I'm gon' say yeah."

Her skin turned red as she smirked at me. "Come on, silly."

She pulled me from my seat, and we held hands to the swings. When Cassie saw her, she nearly lost her mind. She ran to Kendall and hugged her tightly. They both sat in the swings, so I stood behind them, taking turns pushing the both of them. The higher Cassie went, the more she squealed. I couldn't help but have a smile on my face. I was enjoying being around Kendall. She was screaming and laughing as much as Cassie and I couldn't help but hope she would be willing to give us a try. I was already going against my original decision.

I'd said I would leave her alone and let her come back to me when she was ready, but shit, I couldn't stop thinking about her. My mind wouldn't let me stop thinking about her. My body didn't want to let go. And my heart... the minute she offered to help take care of my baby, she had the soft side of it. When they'd gotten tired of swinging, we went to the slides and we raced, since it was three-in-one. After that, I was done with squeezing myself into child sized spaces. I walked back to the picnic table I was at and watched them continue playing.

Almost twenty minutes later, Kendall joined me, practically out of breath. I chuckled as she laughed, too. "Shit. Cassie almost made me forget I was thirty-three years old. My body reminded me quick as hell, though."

She was in perfect shape, so she was tripping. "I'm twenty-eight and I sat down a long time ago."

She smiled at me and our gazes locked. I grabbed her hand. It was like I couldn't be around her without touching her in some way. "Look. I tried to convince myself that I wouldn't press. That I would let you make all the moves. But I can't do that. At least, can we get to know one another and decide later if we wanna take this further?"

She looked away, toward Cassie, then turned back to me. "So, no commitment, just talking."

"Yeah, for now."

I rubbed my thumb across the top of her hand as I stared at her. She was nervous and I could feel the tremble through her hand. After clearing her throat, she looked up at me and we seemed to get lost in one another. I didn't know who we were trying to fool, but the shit between us was so damn strong. It was hard to stay focused. Finally parting her lips, she said, "I'd like that."

I pulled her closer to me and put my arm around her shoulder. She leaned her head against me. "You smell good, Price. You always smell good."

"Man, I stink. After you and Cassie had me running around this park."

She giggled. "So, did you always wanna be a truck driver?"

"Naw. I was going to the university for chemistry when Shayla got pregnant with Cassie. I had to do something quick, so I could make more money than what I was making. So, I went to LIT to the truck driving school. It was a six-week program. I was nineteen years old and I been doing this ever since."

"Chemistry. Wow."

"Yeah. I used to love watching those mad scientist shows. You always wanted to be a teacher?"

"Nope. I wanted to be an actress."

"Damn. You would have made a beautiful one. That's for sure. Why didn't you follow through?"

She shrugged her shoulders. "I guess it was self-doubt."

"Well, I'm glad you're open to our possibilities."

"Price. Can I tell you something?"

"You can tell me anything."

"You've had my attention since day one; that Thursday you dropped Cassie to school."

"Same here."

We continued to talk, learning more about one another as Cassie had the time of her life. When I decided to check the time, I realized we'd been at the park for three hours. Before I could say a word to Kendall, her phone started to ring. She looked at it, then silenced it. When she looked over at me, I remembered I needed to tell her I was off. "My dispatcher called and said my load got canceled for tomorrow, so I'm off. Did the two of you have plans already?"

"My parents' are barbecuing. I was gonna bring her with me. Everyone is expecting to meet the little girl that has my heart already."

"Her daddy wants to have your heart eventually, too. But I'll wait patiently. So, I know you don't want me to meet your parents. I'll be cool by myself for a little while, since they're excited about meeting her."

Her phone rang again, and she silenced it. I stood to my feet and pulled her to hers. We stood facing each other and I couldn't help the shit, but I had to taste her lips. I lowered my head and lightly pecked them, then licked my lips. It was hot outside, but my body temperature was scorching. My dick started to wake up a bit, so I knew I had to separate myself from her before I wanted more. "Price, that felt good and your lips barely touched mine."

"I've been wanting to kiss your lips and I want more, but I don't wanna give Cassie a show. She already telling me to shoot my shot."

She looked up at me as her eyes widened. A laugh escaped her. "I think she's been trying to hook us up. She told me you like me, and that she knew I liked you, too."

"That lil girl..." I shook my head slowly, then called for Cassie so we could leave. "Well, I'm gonna go. I'm tired and I need a bath."

The vision of her being naked came to my mind, but I quickly dismissed it. "Aight."

"I'll see you tomorrow. Kiss Cassie for me."

"Okay. If I have to go get her, it won't be pretty."

She giggled, then kissed my cheek. As I watched all that ass walk away from me, Cassie appeared at my side. "So, how did it go?"

"We're getting to know one another."

"Good job, Daddy."

I side-eyed her as we made our way to the truck to head to Dairy Queen. Kendall Washington... whether she knew it or not, she was mine. This talking phase would be for nothing, because I wasn't seeing anybody else. Thinking about those flowers on her desk, I hoped she wasn't seeing anybody else either.

CHAPTER 9

K endall

When I woke up, it was the next morning. I'd had an amazing time at the park with Cassie and Price, but I was tired as hell. I had ten missed calls from West. I rolled my eyes. He was being extra clingy now. We weren't a couple. Damn! Two dates and about three phone conversations. That was it. I decided to call him back though, because I didn't need him interrupting me today. He'd done enough of that yesterday. I couldn't believe I'd given Price the okay. When his lips touched mine, I thought I was gonna pull him in for more. They were so damn soft. Thinking about him had me all sidetracked until my phone chimed, alerting me of a text message.

I grabbed it from my nightstand, fully expecting it to be West. My mind was in "go the fuck off" mode until I saw Price's name. It melted the ice, when I read, *Good morning, beautiful. Can't wait to see you.*

I smiled big as hell. Everything about him turned me on. He was so open and gentle with me. I could tell that he could be rough and demanding as well, but that wasn't what he showed me yesterday. He gave me a softer side of him. I responded, *Good morning, handsome. I can't wait to see you either.*

Looking at the time, I saw it was only eight, but I decided to call West anyway. He didn't give a damn about calling me at one this morning. He'd better be glad my phone was on 'do not disturb' and didn't wake me up. He would have gotten a whole 'notha Kendall. I hated being disturbed while I was sleeping... unless, it was worth my while to wake up. The phone rang a couple of times, before he finally answered groggily. "Hello?"

"Is there an emergency, West?"

"Huh?"

I rolled my eyes. "You called me ten times between yesterday evening and one o'clock this morning."

"I'm sorry, Kendall. I guess I was just nervous about losing you before I even got you. I just wanted to make sure everything was still cool between us and when you didn't answer by the second phone call or return my call within an hour, I panicked. Again, I apologize."

I rolled my eyes once again and exhaled. "West, I told you yesterday that we were cool. I don't say things I don't mean. We're cool. So, chill out."

"Okay. Well, I go back to work tomorrow, so hopefully I can see you this evening before you turn in for the night."

Against my better judgement, I said, "That's possible, West. I'll call you later."

"Okay."

I ended the call and stared at the ceiling. This would probably be the last time I entertained him. I didn't see how some women dated two men at once. West was starting to wear on my damn nerves already. I got up and started the shower. Price and Cassie would be meeting me here at ten, so I needed to be ready to head out. My parents had a huge gathering every Labor Day. It was mostly family that came, but it was still huge. The Washington clan ran deep.

I was sure to moisturize my skin with my scented lotion. Price seemed to be the affectionate type and would most likely want a hug. I wanted more than a hug, but for the sake of Cassie, I knew we needed to get to know one another a little more before we crossed into unchartered territory. While I knew the basics, like his age, occupation, and even about his immediate family, I needed to know his inner workings. Things that made him tick and the things that angered him the most were some things I wouldn't necessarily get from conversation.

After getting dressed in a cute romper and putting on my sandals, the doorbell rang. I slid some gloss on my lips, then ran down the hallway to answer the door. When I opened it, Cassie nearly jumped in my arms. "Hey, Ms. Washington!"

"Hi, baby!"

I had the biggest smile on my face and when I looked up at Price, I noticed he did, too. "Hey, Kendall."

"Hey, Price. Come on in."

Cassie had made herself comfortable on the couch and had turned on the TV. I led Price to the kitchen island, so we could have a little privacy. "How was your night?" he asked.

"When I came home and had bathed, I went to sleep and didn't wake up until this morning."

His eyebrows had risen, causing me to giggle. "You were really tired."

"Yeah."

He grabbed my hand, which seemed to be something he liked to do. I liked it, too. His touch gave me goosebumps and I couldn't wait to experience that touch in other places. My eyes met his and it was like they were hooked. He tilted his head. "What are thinking, Kendall?"

I swallowed hard. "Just about how I seem to get drawn into your stare and how your touch feels amazing."

What did I say that shit for? Price smiled, then rested his other hand on my knee. My legs parted and I knew that his touch was dangerous. They didn't spread wide open, but when he touched me, I could no longer hold them closed. He noticed. Looking down at my legs, he pulled his bottom lip into his mouth. "So, what time do I need to pick up Cassie?"

My lips parted, but nothing came out. This man had me dumb. Once I got caught up in him, my ass couldn't focus. He glanced over at Cassie, then laid his lips on mine. I wasn't wearing a bra and I could feel my nipples hardening even more than they already were. He gently sucked my bottom lip as he pulled away and a soft moan left my lips. Price continued to stare at me, then ran his fingertips down my arm. "My brother won't be back until Thursday, because his father-in-law's funeral is tomorrow. Can Cassie ride home with you tomorrow and Wednesday?"

Breaking from my trance, I said, "Of course. And umm... you can pick her up around six. I plan to be home no later than that."

"Aight. Well, I guess I better go, so y'all can get going."

I lifted my hand to his face and rubbed it over his beard. The hair wasn't long enough to grab, and thankfully, it hindered me from going too far. My hands would have grabbed that hair and pulled him back to my lips. I dropped my head and took a couple of deep breaths. Price stood from his stool, then pulled me from mine and pulled me in his arms. *Damn, he smelled so good.* I laid my head on his chest as Cassie looked back at us with a smile on her face. Lifting my head, I said, "Sorry."

"Don't worry about it. When my brother gets back, we can have some private time to enjoy moments like this."

I nodded in response. I couldn't wait to feel his tongue glide against mine. Price was threatening to unravel me at every turn, and it was becoming more difficult to contain myself. Grabbing my hand, he led me to the door. "See y'all at six. If y'all get back earlier, call me."

"Okay. What are you gonna do?"

"Chill out at home and wish I was with y'all."

He gave me a slight smile, then kissed my lips and walked to his truck. I watched him until he'd driven away. "I'm glad y'all like each other, because then I can be with both of you at the same time," Cassie said, standing next to me while waving at her daddy.

I gave her smile. "Let's go."

~

"She's so cute, Ken Ken."

"Yes, she is. She's a sweetheart, too, Mama."

"I gathered that when she hugged me. What do her parents think about the liking you've taken to their daughter?"

"Well... her mama disappeared about a month ago, so she lives with her dad."

My mother's eyebrows had risen. Brenda Washington wasn't for bullshit and games. She peeped shit right off. I knew this about her, so I didn't know why I brought Cassie, other than I loved having her around me. "So, what does he say about your relationship with Cassie?"

"It's... uh..."

"You like him, don't you?"

"Yeah. But it wasn't before I took a liking to Cassie. I didn't meet him until this past Thursday. That was only because I'd written him a note about needing to speak with him about her hair."

"Let me guess. It was all over the place."

My mama chuckled as did I. "Yes."

"Well, I'm not one to judge, baby. You should have invited him, too."

"We aren't serious. We just agreed yesterday to get to know one another. I wasn't ready to have him here in this environment."

"This environment meaning, nosy ass relatives. I get that."

I chuckled again as Cassie came inside. "Ms. Washington, can I have some water?"

"Of course, baby. There's a cooler outside right by the door."

"Oh! Thank you."

"You're welcome."

"I hope things work out for y'all, because she loves you," my mama said after Cassie walked out.

"Yeah. I love her, too."

The rest of the day had gone well. Cassie enjoyed playing with all the kids and the huge game of dodgeball that we played every year. My mind had been somewhat distant though, because I swore this car was following me. I could be paranoid at times, so I tried to brush it off, but it kept popping in my head. If I ever noticed that car again, I'd know that it wasn't a coincidence. Price had texted once to see how our day was going. I'd sent him pictures of Cassie having the time of her life.

At four, I decided to go ahead and leave. It was hot as hell and I was glad I had braided our hair this past weekend. My hair would have been a frizzy mess from the humidity. Once Cassie hugged everyone and promised to come back to visit as if that would be her decision, we headed back to my house. I called Price to let him know we were heading back, and he sounded excited. After he left, I knew the little time I gave West today would be to break it off with him. I wanted to spend all my free time with Price and Cassie. While we weren't exclusive, I knew we eventually would be.

As I turned in my driveway, I saw that car pass by. I hadn't noticed it on my way home, but to see it pass by my house made me nervous as hell. Tomorrow, I'd try to get a plate number if I saw it again. After getting inside the house, I sat on the couch and took in the cool air. I didn't live too far from my parents, so by the time the car cooled off, I was home. Cassie sat next to me. "Thank you, Ms. Washington. I had fun."

"Me too. But it was soooo hot!"

She giggled and I did as well. Not long after, the doorbell rang. I knew it was Price, so I ran to it, only to open the door and see West standing there. *What the fuck was he on?* I frowned as he smiled at me. "I was in the neighborhood and decided to stop and see if you had made it home yet. I went to a barbecue a couple of blocks away."

"Well, I wish you would have called first. Cassie is with me and I don't want to have her around you."

He frowned. "What do you mean?"

"West, I don't fully trust you because I don't know you like that. I can't have someone else's daughter around you without their knowledge."

Before I could respond, I saw Price turn in the driveway and park right behind West. *Oh shit.* The frown on Price's face made me slightly tremble. I hoped he didn't think this was what it looked like. "West, I was going to cut you off today. I planned to call you once Cassie's dad picked her up. Now, this is going to look shady to him."

When Price walked up, he stood next to West and held out his hand to offer a handshake. While they shook, that frown was still in place. I grabbed Price's hand and West's eyebrows shot up. "Oh, so you seeing your charity case."

What the fuck! "Who the fuck do you think you are? I never said anything like that to you."

Price had turned red and he grabbed the doorknob and closed the door. His icy glare was on me, then he turned to West. "You can go fuck yourself dude. I don't know you and you don't know me. I will fuck yo' ass up, no questions asked. But obviously, Kendall been running her damn mouth about me and mine." He turned to me; the anger evident in his eyes. "So, for future references, I'll remember to handle shit on my own. I'll find a beautician for Cassie."

My heart was crushed. I wasn't telling his business. Grabbing Price's arm to try to explain, he glared at me, causing me to release his arm quickly. When he opened the door again, a calm seemed to come over him. "Cassie, come on, baby."

"Price, I did not talk about you or Cassie to him. I only said that I would have Cassie today. That's it."

"Aight."

He was fuming and I knew he was trying to be calm in front of Cassie. When she got to the door, she had a smile on her face until she looked at West's ass. Had Price not blocked him in, I would hope he would have left by now. "Bye, Ms. Washington," she said softly.

"Bye, sweetheart."

As I leaned over to hug her, Price walked off, pulling her with him. She looked back at me as she walked, and those eyes pleaded with me to not let them go. I closed my door and ran past West to Price's truck. I stood in front of his door. "Price, this is not what it looks like. He popped up without an invitation. He only knew that Cassie and I were spending time together, because he'd wanted to spend time with me Saturday and today. I know that I want you and not him and had planned to tell him so. I never expected him to show up here."

The entire time I spoke, he looked around to avoid looking at me. When I finished talking, he looked in my eyes and what I saw made my heart beat erratically. He looked hurt and angry. "Can you move, so we can leave? You do still have company that had I not gotten here sooner, might had been around my daughter."

I slowly stepped out of his way, trying to plead with my eyes, similar to the way Cassie had done to me. I blew a kiss at her and I saw her crying. That broke my heart. This was what I was trying to avoid. However, whether we were talking or not, this would have been a big misunderstanding. I could kill West. As Price drove away, I felt West put his arm around me. I immediately turned to him and slapped the fuck out of him. "Get the fuck off my property before I call the police."

He looked stunned that I'd popped him, but he could look stunned all he wanted to. I should've punched him in his got damn throat. He bit his bottom lip like he wanted do or say something. After rubbing his face for a second, he frowned and the muthafucka looked like he was about to growl like dog. While my insides were trembling, I stood my ground as he nodded and got in his car. When he drove away, I exhaled and went inside, then tried to call Price. The phone only rang, then went to voicemail. I sat on my couch and for the first time in a long time, I cried.

CHAPTER 10

P rice

I WAS SO ANGRY. I could have killed Kendall and that nigga. My baby cried all the way home. When Kendall called, I had to ignore her call, or I would have cursed her ass out. Before we could get out the truck, I turned to my baby. "I'm sorry, Cassie."

"Who was he?"

"I don't know, and I wasn't trying to stick around to find out. If you want me to, I'll request the school transfer you to another teacher."

"No. I love Ms. Washington. She said it wasn't her fault, Daddy."

I no longer wanted to have the conversation, because thinking about Kendall was irritating me. I didn't ask for her help. She offered. "Come on, Cassie."

We got out of the truck and Cassie was walking across the parking lot when my biggest fear flashed before my eyes. "Cassie!"

A pickup truck came out of nowhere and plowed into my baby.

Her body flew at least forty feet as he slammed on his breaks. I screamed as I ran to her. Several of us parents had been complaining about how fast vehicles were flying through the parking lot and how they needed to have speed bumps installed. He had to be going at least thirty miles per hour when he should have only been going ten at the max. I ran to her and she was unconscious, but still breathing. I immediately called 9-1-1, screaming into the phone. Cradling my baby in my arms was all I could think to do, but I didn't want to move her. The damage her body could have suffered was taking over my thought processes. "Cassie, please stay with me. Hang on, baby," I said while crying.

People had begun to gather around us, and some were crying as much as I was. Had my baby not been as injured as she was, I would have fucked ol' dude up, but I couldn't be concerned with him right now. I lightly rubbed Cassie's head as I laid next to her, pleading with God to spare my child. I kissed her cheek over and over as I noticed the blood coming from underneath her. I felt helpless, watching her face swell until she was no longer recognizable. "Stay with me, Cassie. Listen to Daddy's voice, baby. Hang on."

For what seemed like took forever, I finally heard the ambulance sirens blaring as the people dispersed to allow them through. I felt like I was losing her, and that feeling was too much to bear. After they slid the board under her and lifted her body to the gurney, we all ran to the ambulance. Watching them poke my baby with needles and move so quickly to get her stabilized was killing me. She was strong, but her body looked so fragile. But the fact that she was hanging on, gave me hope.

When they informed me that they would be life flighting her to Texas Children's Hospital in Houston, I was somewhat relieved. She would receive better care there. However, nothing would relieve the sadness, anxiety, and anger that I felt about what happened. Once they'd stabilized her, I was allowed to sit next to her. Her nose was broken, and she had head trauma. I couldn't lose my baby. She probably couldn't open her eyes even if she wanted to as swollen as her face was. At this point, I didn't want her to be awake to feel all the pain. I was almost sure she had a few broken bones.

As I heard the helicopter, I sent my brother a message. *Cassie was hit by a truck. They are life flighting her to Texas Children's Hospital in Houston. I'll call you when I get there and know more.*

I wanted to call Kendall, but at the same time, I didn't have time to deal with what had happened today. Once I had time, I would call the school and they would alert her to what had happened. I then sent a message to my job, letting them know that I would be out indefinitely. There was no way I could go to work as long as my baby was in the hospital and I couldn't expect them to hold my job until I was able to return. I didn't even know how long I would be off.

Once it landed, I was informed that I couldn't ride, that I would have to drive. That shit nearly tore me up. How in the hell was I gonna drive by myself, thinking about my baby? I didn't have time to question or argue with anybody. I needed to get there fast so I could know what was going on with Cassie. After kissing her head, I whispered in her ear, "Everything's gon' be okay, baby. Daddy will be right there with you. I love you so much, Cassie. So, I need you to be strong and fight. I don't ever want to be without you."

"Okay. Let's go!" the paramedic said.

I moved quickly, hopping out and running to my truck. When I got inside, I watched them run with her on the gurney as fast as they could against the wind from the blades of the helicopter. As I sat there, I fell apart. I wanted to ask God, *why my baby?* I tried to do everything I was supposed to do. I was good to people. Why my daughter? As I unraveled in my truck, I prayed that God would spare her life. Starting my truck, I took off for IH-10 West. Hopefully a cop didn't get behind me or his ass was gon' have to follow me all the way to Texas Children's Hospital.

As I sped down the interstate, I could only think about how happy Cassie had been this weekend. That then led my thoughts to Kendall. Did I really want her to find out through the school? Regardless of what happened today, I knew she loved Cassie. Grabbing my phone from the console as I trembled, I called her, then put it down as it rang through the Bluetooth. "Hello?"

"Kendall."

"Hi. I really am sorry about what happened."

"I'm on my way to Houston. Cassie was hit by a truck and they are life flighting her to Texas Children's."

"What? You can't be serious."

I could hear her voice quivering and that did nothing for the tears I was trying to hold back. "He hit my baby, Kendall. I'm trying to hold it together and be strong, but she doesn't look good. She was so swollen and looked lifeless. How am I going to go through life without her if God decides to take her?"

The tears were falling uncontrollably, and for a moment, I thought I was going to have to stop. I quickly wiped my face and pulled myself together. Time wasn't something I had the luxury of having, so I refused to waste any of it sitting on side of the road, crying. She was crying, too. "I wish I was there with you, but I will be there soon. I'm getting dressed now. I'll call my principal so she can get me a sub. You don't have to go through this alone, Price."

I couldn't respond to her verbally, because I didn't want to start crying again. I'd made it to Winnie in twenty minutes and that was normally a thirty-minute trip. Hopefully, I'd continue to make good time. "I'm going to stay on the phone with you until you get there. Even if you don't say a word, I'll be on the line in case you want to. Okay?"

"Okay."

I could hear her moving around quite a bit, then within minutes her car started. She was on her way to me. Once I got situated and found out about Cassie, I'd call Karter back. I stared straight ahead and focused my energy on driving and praying aloud. Kendall was doing the same. He couldn't let her die. He just couldn't.

I PACED BACK and forth in the waiting area and I couldn't manage to sit down until I knew something. When I'd gotten here, everyone seemed to know about Cassie and had helped me get to where I needed to be. They had immediately taken Cassie into surgery and I couldn't take it. Kendall had talked to me until I'd gotten inside the hospital. I'd turned a one and half hour drive into one hour flat and thankfully, I didn't get stopped, especially being that it was Labor Day. When I got off the phone with her, she was twenty minutes away.

I'd already been here for fifteen minutes. When someone came into the waiting area and said Daniels family, I ran to her. She said, "Is it just you?"

"Yes ma'am."

I anxiously followed behind her to a private consultation room. "Are you her father?"

"Yes."

"Okay. The doctor will be in here in a moment, along with other personnel, so you can sign more paperwork. Do you need anything? Water? Coffee?"

"No thanks."

She nodded and left the room. I was starting to panic. *Why did they put me in this private consultation room?* In Beaumont, when they did that, it was because they didn't expect your loved one to make it. My chiming phone took me from my thoughts. It was Kendall. I told her to just give Cassie's name, then told her that I was in the private consultation room. As I paced back and forth, my head was pounding. I didn't know what to expect. When the door opened, I was expecting to see Kendall, but it was the doctor. He had a solemn look on his face, so I closed my eyes. "Just tell me."

"She is still in surgery, but it doesn't look good. Her body was nearly crushed. Almost every bone in her body seemed to break. However, her neck and spine are still good. She has a lot of swelling on her brain, along with bleeding and one of her lungs has collapsed. We are doing everything we can for your angel. Once she comes out of surgery, we will be keeping her sedated. With her being as young as she is, feeling that amount of pain could send her into shock."

"Could she eventually make a full recovery?"

"In my professional experience, I would say she has maybe a ten percent chance of totally recovering from this. It's not impossible. If she can pull through this week, that percentage will go up. I hate to see this, especially for a baby."

"I pray she does."

"I'll be praying with you. How old is she?"

"Eight."

"Okay. I'm gonna go back in there. We're looking at maybe another three hours. Someone will be updating you throughout the process. Again, we brought you in this room, because it doesn't look good, but with our prayers, we can believe for a miracle."

He sat his hand on my shoulder and squeezed, then headed out. Just as I sat, Kendall stood in the doorway. When she entered the room and closed the door, I stood back up. She ran to me and hugged me tightly around the neck. I hugged her just as tightly. When she pulled away, she put her hands to my face. "What did they say? Why are you in this room?"

"Let me call my brother and I'll tell you both at the same time. I don't think I can bear to say it more than once, right now."

She nodded her head as I made the call. "Hello?"

"Hey, Karter."

"What are they saying, bruh? How are you holding up?"

"I'm barely hanging on, man. The doctor said almost every bone in her body was broken. That truck crushed her, bruh." I allowed the tears to flow and my breathing to get labored for a moment. "Her brain is swollen and bleeding. The only good news was that her spine and neck seemed to be okay. She's still in surgery and he said she would be for probably the next three hours. Karter, I'm so scared. I can't lose my daughter."

"I'm so sorry, Price. But listen. We not losing Cassie. You hear me? We not losing baby girl. God wouldn't give her to us, just to take her. I can't believe that he would allow something like that."

"I've been praying. I can't go through this again. Losing Mama and Daddy hurt, but this... Cassie... I wouldn't make it."

"I know. But get that out your head. She gon' make it."

"I have to go, Karter. I'll keep you updated."

"Okay. We'll be there Friday when the kids get out of school. Love you, bruh."

"Aight. I love you, too."

After ending the call, I sat on the couch and allowed my head to rest against the wall. Kendall grabbed my hand and held it between hers as she cried softly. She rested against me and I dropped my arm around her shoulders, glad that she was even here. Life was like a vapor, but I continued to pray within my spirit that Cassie's life would continue beyond my own. No parent wanted to bury their child and I prayed God wouldn't make me have to do that.

CHAPTER 11

K endall

WHEN I WOKE UP, I realized that I wasn't dreaming. I was in a live nightmare. Cassie had been hit by a truck and I didn't know how I would move on from this if she didn't make it. If I felt that way after only knowing her for two weeks, I could only imagine how Price was feeling. Her infectious smile and laugh made anyone that came in contact with her, love her. Listening to the doctor that was speaking with Price, I heard him say that they nearly lost her, but were able to revive her. He also said that she lost a kidney, had a liver laceration, a ruptured spleen, and that they had to remove her gall bladder.

I immediately rushed to Price's side, because he looked as if he was gonna lose it. Hugging him around his waist, I could feel his body trembling. I laid my head on his back, trying to emotionally hold him up. He needed to know that no matter how weak I was feeling, I was here for him. "Don't be in despair Mr. Daniels. None of that is a death sentence. Remember, we're praying right?" the doctor said as he placed his hand on Price's shoulder.

"Yes, sir. Thank you."

The doctor smiled. "Next time I come back, we should be done. They'll take her to recovery, then ICU. You'll be able to see her once they've gotten her situated. Oh, we'll also need to get blood from you. That will be ideal for Cassie to have your blood."

"Okay."

The doctor left out and Price turned around in my arms and hugged me. He kissed my head. "Thank you for being here, Kendall. I'm sorry for earlier. I know you wouldn't do what he made it seem like you did. I at least know that much about you. I know you love Cassie."

"Thank you for sharing her with me. I do love her. I never would have thought that West would flip the script on me like that. But that situation is dead. There's only one man I want to entertain. So, whatever you need from me, you got that shit."

I knew that we were both feeling sensitive and vulnerable, but I never expected him to lay his lips on mine, blessing me with the most passion filled and gentlest kiss I'd ever had. My entire body shivered, and I wanted more. His hands slid down my back and rested on my hips before he pulled away. He only stared in my eyes, not saying a word. Leading me to the couch, we both sat. Shortly after, a nurse came to get him so they could get blood from him. That left me in the consultation room alone in my thoughts.

Looking at the time to see that it was already ten, I called my mama. "Hello?"

"Hey, Mama."

"What's wrong, Ken Ken?"

"Cassie got hit by a truck..." I said, letting my emotions free that I'd tried to contain. "She's in surgery. That truck crushed her, Mama. We're praying for a miracle."

"Oh my God, baby. Where are you?"

"I'm in Houston with her dad at Texas Children's. They're getting blood from him for when she needs it."

"Lord, I'm so sorry to hear this."

I could hear the emotion in my mom's voice. She'd only met Cassie today, but anything like this happening to anyone, let alone a child, pulled on everyone's heartstrings. We talked a little longer as I gave her details and asked her to let Alana and P know. I laid on the couch just as a nurse entered with two pillows and two blankets. I didn't know how she knew, but I was thankful. The blanket was warm, and once I covered up with it, I went back to sleep.

Not long after I'd dozed off, my phone was ringing. I wanted to cry. Sleep was hard to come by with what was going on and I knew after this, I probably wouldn't be able to go back to sleep. It was my principal, though. "Hello?"

"Hi, Ms. Washington. I just wanted you to know that we want to do a fundraiser for Cassie and her dad and possibly a go fund me page. We know he probably won't be working and will need food and other things while Cassie is in the hospital. Could you ask him, if he would be okay with us advertising this on the news? I know how men can be about receiving help, but we all want to. This situation is tragic, and we don't want him to have to be worried about finances while he's with his daughter."

"That's so sweet. I'll ask him. They took him to give blood."

"Okay. And umm... Are y'all seeing each other?"

I lowered my head as if she could see me. I didn't think this went against any type of moral clause in my contract. However, I didn't want to lose Cassie as my student. I suppose at this point, it really didn't matter. "Yes, ma'am. That just happened this weekend, actually."

"Okay. While I'm sure Cassie won't be returning to school for a while, we'll have to transfer her to another class. She probably won't be back this school year. Are you going to home school her?"

"I hadn't thought about that yet, but I would love to when she gets to that point. So she won't fall behind."

"Okay, sweetie. I'll let you go. I'll also call tomorrow some time to check on Cassie. Text me and let me know what her dad says."

"I will."

After ending the call, I sat there and pondered how I would ask Price about what we'd talked about. The fact that West's stupid ass had called him a charity case earlier, I knew that subject would be touchy. As I waited for him to return, I began scrolling Facebook and noticed I had a message through messenger. It was from West. *Shit!* Before I'd left home, I'd blocked his number so he could no longer call or text me. I didn't think to block his ass on social media. Opening the message, I read his apology. Something had to be mentally wrong with his ass. I proceeded to unfriend him and block his ass without responding. Although, he would be able to tell I'd seen his message. As usual, he was sorry and didn't mean to cause trouble between me and my student's parent. He was so full of shit.

After playing my coloring game to relax my nerves, Price had made it back to the consultation room. "You okay?"

"Yeah. Just a little weak. They said they were just about done in surgery and would most likely be able to give her my blood within the hour. They had to run tests for compatibility, but of course, we should be a match. I'm B positive and she should be the same or at least a compatible variant with me and her mom's genes."

"Speaking of her mom, do you know how to get in touch with her to let her know what has happened?"

"The number I've been calling goes straight to voicemail and the box is full. She made it perfectly clear after a week of no return phone calls that she didn't want Cassie anymore. Triflin' bitch." He glanced over at me. "Sorry."

He didn't have to apologize to me. In this situation, he could call her a bitch all day and it wouldn't faze me. She was a bitch and a bunch of other things for abandoning her child the way she did. If she didn't want to be a parent anymore, there was a better way of doing that. In my book, she was a ratchet, stupid ass bitch. How could anybody leave Cassie? She was such a beautiful and respectable child. She had manners that I had to assume had been taught to her by Price. "It's okay. What about any other family?"

"It's just me and Karter. That's it."

"Okay."

I could tell that the subject was starting to irritate him. He began telling me how they'd already given Cassie blood when she first got there, because she'd lost quite a bit, but they would have his blood for when they needed it. With the liver laceration, she could lose blood rather quickly, so they would have enough blood on hand. I grabbed Price's hand. "You want something to eat? Coffee?"

"Naw, thanks. I can't eat right now, and I don't drink coffee."

"Okay. What about tea? I'm gonna go make me a cup."

"Naw. Thanks."

I kissed his cheek, then left out of the room, only to see a female frantically looking for someone. Upon eye contact, I knew it was her. She was the grownup version of Cassie. My tea was no longer a priority. This chick looked like she could be a handful and if I had to knock her ass out, I would. She wasn't about to come in here talking crazy to Price. She walked over to me and said, "My name is Shayla Corbin. Cassie Daniels is my daughter. For some reason, I feel like you can help me."

"Price is in the consultation room."

Bitch, please. She felt like I could help her. The bitch had put two and two together. I was staring at her ass. Secondly, she saw me walk out of that consultation room. Price had to be in there if he was nowhere else. She nodded her head and walked in that direction with me right next to her. When she walked in, Price's face turned about three different shades of red. He stood from his seat and it looked like he wanted to beat the shit out of her. I stood between them. "Price what happened?"

"Oh, you actually give a fuck? I thought you were too busy having a fucking hot girl summer."

She lowered her head. "Shit, Price! I feel bad enough about it. What happened to Cassie?"

She was almost screaming, and for a milli-second, I felt sorry for her. "She was hit by a truck crossing the parking lot at the apartment complex."

"You weren't watching her, Price? Why would you let her cross by herself?"

It took every ounce of strength in my body to keep Price from grabbing her by the neck. I put my hands to his cheeks and forced him to look at me. "Please, calm down, Price. Think about Cassie. Nothing else matters."

"Who are you?" Shayla asked.

I turned around to stare her in the face. She was maybe an inch shorter than me and she was maybe a size bigger than me. "I'm Price's girlfriend and I used to be Cassie's teacher."

"Price, when you get a girlfriend? After me, you couldn't seem to keep one."

"Man, why the fuck you here?"

"I came to check on Cassie!"

"Sound like you here checking for me. You can get the fuck outta here with that shit. Cassie in there fighting for her life and you in here on some fucking bullshit. You ain't been around for a whole fucking month. No calls, texts, or nothing. Like you just dropped off the face of the fucking earth. But now you got the nerve to come in here questioning me about my baby? You wanna get fucked up. And we got a court date next week for the child abandonment charges I filed against you."

Shit. I couldn't move. Price had me and her on pause. Finally, she found her voice and asked, "How is she?"

"You see where you standing? She ain't doing good, Shay."

She sat in a chair across from us and I watched the tears stream down her cheeks. "I felt like I was suffocating. I couldn't go nowhere or do what I wanted to do, because I always had to look out for Cassie. I never got a chance to enjoy being an adult. I was eighteen when I got pregnant and nineteen when I had her. Now that I don't know if she's gonna make it or not, I feel selfish as hell. What was I thinking?"

"That's the problem. You wasn't thinking."

We sat there in silence for a little while and I held Price's hand in mine, doing my best to stay quiet. Their exchange had rubbed me raw. She was tired of being a mother and here I was wishing I'd eventually get to be one. I glanced at her a couple of times, only to find her looking at me from head to toe. I was praying I didn't have to show this bitch that just because I was a teacher didn't mean I wouldn't fuck her up. As we all continued to sit there quietly, the doctor walked in. "We made it through."

We all sighed in relief as he continued. "The next few days are critical. She has some internal bleeding, due to the liver laceration and she has a lot of swelling. I'm hoping we won't have to relieve it and that it goes down on its own. There's also a slight problem. Can I speak with you privately, Mr. Daniels?"

Price glanced at me, then Shayla, and said, "Yes."

"Wait! I'm her mother. I should be a part of this conversation as well."

"Yes ma'am," the doctor said nervously.

I didn't know what was going on, but I was praying that everything would be okay. It was quiet for a while, then there was a loud bang against the door. "You bitch!" I heard Price almost scream.

He was crying. I went to the door and opened it to see Price being restrained by a security guard and Shayla sitting on the floor. I walked over to him, my heart beating erratically. "Price, what's going on?"

"The doctor just told me that I wasn't Cassie's biological father. My baby needs blood and I can't give it to her, because for almost nine years, this bitch lied to me, making me believe she was mine."

"Price. She's yours. Blood doesn't matter. That's your baby."

"Well, in this case, blood does matter. It's what matters the most right now."

I wanted to go over there and kick Shayla in her damn mouth. How would Price recover from this? I was scared for him. Shayla could choose to take Cassie and there wouldn't be a thing he could do about it. At least to my knowledge. Maybe if he'd signed the birth certificate, he'd have a dog in the fight. I felt sick inside for him, and I just prayed that things would calm down before it was time to see Cassie.

CHAPTER 12

P rice

My heart felt like it had been put through a fucking shredder. To know that Cassie wasn't mine, had me feeling low. I couldn't seem to function. When the doctor told me, I almost choked the hell out of Shayla against the door. I'd grabbed her by her neck and slammed her against the shit. My heart just felt like it was torn in two. After the security guard grabbed me, I felt even lower for putting my hands on a woman. I'd never been so angry and hurt all at the same damn time. How was I supposed to explain to my baby that she wasn't mine? While I knew she was mine, she wasn't. Cassie was another man's seed.

Security had made Shayla go to another waiting area after the doctor told them the situation. I was thankful they didn't call the police and have me arrested. I'd apologized to the doctor and the staff for my behavior and thanked them for understanding. As I sat there, waiting to see Cassie, Kendall rubbed my back. I hadn't spoken a word to her since I told her what happened. I could tell that she was nervous, not knowing how to approach me with conversation, so she stayed silent. First the wreck, now this. Why was God allowing all this? Did he not think I was worthy of the beautiful angel he'd given me?

I slumped in my seat and lifted my hands to my face, allowing more tears to stream down as I silently prayed. I could feel Kendall's eyes on me, so I slid my hands down my face, wiping away my tears, then grabbed her hand. My heart couldn't take the sorrow in her eyes, so I looked away. She'd had my back with Shayla and said she was my girlfriend. If only I hadn't been so worried about Cassie and what this revelation would do to our relationship, I would have smiled and brought up what she'd said. Lifting her hand to my lips, I kissed the back of it. Before she could say anything, the nurse came in. "Mr. Daniels, you can see her now."

I quickly stood from my seat and pulled Kendall up with me. "I'm sorry sir, only two of you can go in at a time."

"It's only two of us."

"Her mother is also wanting to go in."

"She can wait. She abandoned her and hadn't seen her in a month. Plus, I can't be in that room with her."

"Umm... okay. Give me a minute."

"Clearly she didn't see what happened earlier," Kendall said under her breath.

"Right."

After waiting a few minutes longer, she came back. With a small smile, she said, "Okay. Follow me."

When we walked out, I could hear Shayla's ass talking loudly, demanding to see her daughter. I slowly shook my head. Holding Kendall's trembling hand, I prayed that I could keep it together in there. I knew Cassie wasn't conscious, but I didn't want to say or do anything that could hinder her progress. She could possibly still hear everything that would be going on around her. The more we walked, the sicker I felt. What I would see would knock the wind out of me. I already knew that, but it seemed there was nothing I could do to prepare myself for it. As we walked, the nurse slowed her pace and turned to us. "If you need anything, let me know. She's a fighter and we're all fighting with and for her."

I nodded my head and she slid the patio-like door back. When I saw my baby laying there, I nearly crumbled. Tears I didn't think I had left sprang from my eyes as I rushed to her bedside. Looking at all the tubes on her and seeing how swollen she was made me thank God that she was even still alive. Looking at the damage to her body, she should have been dead. I didn't know what lesson God was trying to teach, but he had my undivided attention. I kissed Cassie softly on her head. "Hey, baby girl. Daddy's here. You made it through surgery. You're so strong."

Pausing to sniff and wipe my face, I said, "Daddy loves you. Ms. Washington is here, too. She had to come see about you."

I waved Kendall over as her knees buckled, threatening to send her crashing to the floor. Walking over to her, I wrapped my arms around her and led her to Kendall's bedside. She was quiet for a while. All that could be heard was soft moans and sniffing, as we both cried tears from our souls. My faith was strong, but that didn't stop me from hurting, knowing the road Cassie had ahead. All the rehabilitation she would have to go through, just to try to get back to normal; learning how to walk and talk again, which were some things we took for granted.

Kendall reached out to touch Cassie. She was trembling so much. "Cassie. Hi, sweetheart. I'm here to see about you and to let you know that the entire school is praying for you. I've taken off work the rest of the week to be with you and your dad. I'll have you know that he took his shot, and he scored. He's my boyfriend now."

That made a slight smile come to my face. Cassie wanted me and her teacher to hook up. I looked at her braids and they were a mess. The hospital had to cut them and partially shave her head to stitch the small laceration closed. Her beautiful tresses would have to be cut. We continued to stand there, staring at her body. Suddenly,

Kendall started to sing. I didn't know the song but when she sang the words, *this too shall pass... he'll never give you more than you can bear,* I had to sit down. I broke down. First, I didn't know she could sing, but the words to the song were touching my soul.

Kendall's eyes were closed, and she seemed to be fully engrossed in the lyrics she was singing. I was awe struck with how beautiful her voice was. When she stopped singing, her eyes opened slowly, and she turned to look for me. She walked over to me and I pulled her in my lap. "Thank you, Kendall. That was beautiful."

"You're welcome."

She kissed my cheek, then stood from my lap. I stood and walked back to Cassie's bedside. My body was tired, and I needed to rest. Now that she was out of surgery, maybe I could rest a little bit. Kendall wrapped her arms around my waist. "The school wants to do a fundraiser and start a go fund me for Cassie. They wanted me to ask if you would be okay with that."

I took a deep breath. As proud as I was, I knew I would need the help. Staying here day in and day out with Cassie could get expensive. Not to mention the medical expenses that the insurance wouldn't pay for. I laid my pride to the side and said, "Yeah. I need all the help I can get. Tell them thank you."

Kendall's eyes widened slightly as I pulled a chair to Cassie's bed. I sat next to her and began reading one of her favorite Junie B Jones books from my phone as music from The Descendants played softly. She always liked me to play music as I read. I didn't understand how she could listen to the music and focus on what I was reading to her, but she did. Kendall stood behind me and massaged my shoulders as I read.

A slight groan left my lips as I concentrated on how her touch soothed me physically. Not only was it soothing me physically, it was soothing me mentally, emotionally, and spiritually. When I finished the book, I stood from my seat and decided to try to get some sleep. There was a recliner in the consultation room. They'd said that I could stay in there until they needed it for someone else. Moving the chair back to the corner, I walked back to my baby and kissed her head. "I love you, Cassie. I'm gonna try to get some sleep and me and Ms. Washington will be right back by your side in the morning."

Grabbing Kendall's hand after she kissed Cassie, I pulled her out of the room before I was tempted to stay. I was confident that God was going to pull her out, so I just had to be patient with the process and strong to endure the difficulties on the way. When we got back to the consultation room, I could see Shayla walking with the nurse towards Cassie's room. She looked angry, but I didn't give two fucks on how she felt. When I sat in the recliner, Kendall went to the sofa. "Kendall, come here."

Without hesitation, she stood from the couch and walked over to me. I patted my leg and held my arm out to her. She sat on my lap, then laid on my chest as I reclined the chair. Draping the blanket over us, I kissed her head, then wrapped my arms around her. Feeling her energy and positivity eased my soul and it eased it so much, I went straight to sleep.

~

"WE'RE ON OUR WAY. Tricia didn't want to stay any longer after the funeral. She said we had to get back to check on Cassie."

"Okay, bruh. This hospital can be quite confusing, so ask for help to get to us. How far are y'all away?"

"We just left Jackson a couple of hours ago, but I wanted to get in a groove before I called. Is Shayla still there?"

"She's been coming up here every day, but we aren't in the same area. So, I don't see her, and the staff has been sure to keep us apart."

I'd told him the next day how I almost choked the fuck out of Shayla. We'd been here for three days and there was no change in Cassie's condition. Kendall had gone down to the cafeteria to get us breakfast. Her parents, sister and best friend had all come up to visit Cassie yesterday. It did my heart good to see how much they loved a little girl that they'd just met. And the looks on their faces after they'd seen her was heartbreaking. Cassie had touched everyone's lives that she'd come in contact with, which was more of a reason why I couldn't understand Shayla's decision to leave her.

Cassie had a lot of brain activity, which was good since she had head trauma. They were afraid that had she not had activity, it would have been an even harder battle to fight. The funny thing was that they couldn't explain how she even had any at all. One of the nurses had said that with the type of head trauma Cassie had, her brain should be almost completely dead. The only thing I could say was God was a miracle worker. That alone gave me hope.

When Kendall came back, I helped her to a seat. We were no longer in the consultation room, since a family came in last night. Their loved one had been in a car accident and had been life flighted in as well. "Thank you."

"You're welcome."

Once Kendall had gotten her breakfast prepped where she could eat, I began eating mine. As we ate, I looked over at her. "Kendall, I know it's hard being up here day and night. Why don't you take a break? Get out of here and go shop or get a massage to break up the monotony."

"I will if you will."

I bit my bottom lip. She knew I wasn't leaving Cassie's side, but I didn't expect that same devotion from her. My body was stiff, and I needed a shower something serious. "Okay. Listen. How about I get a hotel room so we can take showers instead of washing off in the bathroom?"

"Okay."

We continued eating in silence. Our days had consisted of sleeping off and on, playing games on our phones and on her iPad, and occasionally talking to family and people calling to check on Cassie. They'd aired the fundraiser on the Beaumont news stations and told the public of the go fund me. They'd already raised ten-thousand and I was more than grateful. Hopefully, I didn't have to get into it with Shayla. I already knew if she found out about that money, she would be thinking that she was entitled to some of it. But she wasn't up here day and night like me and Kendall.

As I got ready to discard my trash, the nurse came to the waiting area looking for us. We nervously walked over to her. "I just wanted you to know that some of the swelling is starting to go down and she opened her eyes. Before we put her back out, I wanted to come get you so she could see you."

My heart was 'bout to burst through my chest as Kendall and I followed her. When we got to the room, I rushed passed the nurse to Cassie and I could see the tears on her face. I kissed her head and all her machines went crazy. Just as fast as we got in there, they pushed us out. Cassie had probably gotten worked up from knowing I was there. Kendall was crying. I pulled her in my arms. "It's okay. This is good. She's responding and getting stronger."

She looked up in my eyes and I kissed her lips. I hated that we hadn't really gotten to let the fact that we were now a couple soak in. As we stood in the hallway, staring at one another, being the comfort that the other needed, the doctor came to us. "Everything is fine. I believe she got excited when you kissed her. We've been keeping her heavily medicated, so she shouldn't be feeling any pain, but of course we don't know that for sure. I wanted to allow her to wake up just to see how she would do. I believe we can gradually wake her up soon. While she still isn't out of the woods, the speed at which she's progressing is miraculous."

"Thank God. When can we see her again? Do we have to wait for visitation?"

"Yes. Visitation is only in an hour. Give us that time to get her situated again. She's feisty."

He chuckled and I did, too. I was seeing that side of her more and more these days. She was pretty quiet around me until Kendall had come into our lives. As we walked out of the ICU unit, Kendall squeezed my hand. "I've never prayed this hard before, Price."

"Me either. And we can't stop just because we've gotten some good news. We gotta keep at it."

"Yes. I hate that I have to go to work Monday."

I put my arm around her shoulder and continued to the waiting area. When we got there, Shayla was sitting on the other side, looking pissed. Hopefully she didn't approach me. I was in a good mood and feeling good about Cassie's progress. But of course, I wasn't so lucky. As we sat, she stood in front of us. "Did something happen with Cassie?"

"She opened her eyes. And some of the swelling has gone down."

She only nodded, then walked away. Well, look at God. He was going to allow me to maintain my peace. I pulled Kendall to me and she rested her head against me. Softly kissing her head, I said in her ear, "I can't wait to show you just how much I'm feeling you. Just the fact that you took this week off work to stay with me and Cassie is overwhelming."

She looked up at me as she rested her hand on my chest. "It's this in here that's so magnetic. Your heart is pure, and I've never witnessed anyone other than my parents, display the type of love you give to Cassie."

I kissed her lips and the way her body shivered in response made me wanna kiss her again. We were in a hospital waiting room, though. She had better get ready, because as soon as Cassie started feeling better, she was gone get months of backed up emotions.

CHAPTER 13

K endall

IT WAS my first day back at work and I was tired as hell. I didn't get home until late last night, because I was trying to spend every minute I possibly could with Price. We'd been taking turns going to the hotel room to shower and his brother had gotten there late Wednesday night. We let them stay in the room we'd gotten, so they didn't have to spend unnecessary money. While it was somewhat impossible to get close to Price the week at the hospital, despite the situation, I was able to feel what it would be like to have his love and affection and that shit was overwhelming.

I'd never been with a man that made me crazy with desire like he had. The absolute craziest part was that I hadn't slept with him. Hadn't felt anything more than his lips on mine and I was all the way in. I couldn't wait to experience more of him, because the sexual tension was thick as hell. His touch was like bolts of electricity that gave my body life. There wasn't a moment that I didn't have goose-bumps around him or feel extremely sensitive.

Cassie's swelling had gone down even more and I was thankful that God was choosing her to work a miraculous healing on. It was so unheard of, that the medical staff had no other way to explain it. She'd had so many visitors over the weekend. Teachers from the school and our principal had all come to visit, along with people that lived in their apartment complex. Price was surprised to see them being that he and Cassie kept to themselves and didn't really know anyone. A few of his coworkers had come as well.

Sitting at my desk, I'd been thinking about Price and Cassie all day. My kids couldn't have learned a thing today. My body was here, but my mind was in Houston at Texas Children's Hospital. I'd been texting Price all day, checking on him and Cassie. While I was missing him, I was also trying to figure out how to handle another issue I was having. On my way to school, I saw that same car following me. I wanted to call the police, but I didn't want to seem like I was overreacting. As I thought about it, I knew it was better to be safe than sorry, so I would call when I got off.

When the kids went to P.E., my phone rang just as I was about to call Price. I went ahead and answered, although I only wanted to talk to him. "Hello?"

The line remained quiet for a second, then I heard, "Hello?"

The blood iced in my veins. "What do you want? I blocked your number. That should be a hint that I no longer wanted to hear from you, West."

"I just wanted a chance to apologize."

"West, you've already done that," I said while rolling my eyes. Before he could respond, a light bulb went off in my head. "Are you following me?"

"What?"

"You heard me, West. Are you following me?"

"Well, someone has to make sure you're safe. You're dating this guy and you don't even know him."

"Just like I didn't know you. I'm regretting every moment we spent together right now. Stop following me! I will call the police."

"Why would you call the police when all I'm doing is trying to make sure you're safe?"

"You're crazy, but guess what? I'm crazy, too. Now stop fucking with me!"

I looked around, remembering where I was and hoping no one had heard me. West was gonna get arrested, because I was calling the police on him before I even left the school. There was no way he could be following me all the time if he was supposed to be at work. He had to have solicited the help of someone else. I just prayed that nothing happened before the police got to him, because it seemed like he was a real mental case. I didn't have time for the foolery.

I ended the call, then called Price as I took deep breaths. When he answered, I was grateful that he sounded upbeat. That meant all was well. "Hey, Kendall. How's your day going?"

"Hey. It's going. I've been wishing I was there all day. How's Cassie?"

"She's doing well. More of the swelling has gone down and it's practically all gone on her head. The internal bleeding is minimal, and her liver has begun healing itself."

"That's great news. Are they gonna wake her up any time soon?"

"This weekend coming. I want you to be here when they do."

My heart. Jesus. "I miss you. How are you?"

"I miss you, too. This past week has spoiled me, but I'm okay."

"What about Shayla?"

"She hasn't come yet today. I don't know if she's coming or not, but I can't be concerned with her. There's only two women I've had my mind on and she isn't one of them."

"Well, besides Cassie, who've you been thinking about?"

"It's this woman that teaches third grade at Mae Jones-Clark Elementary that got that fire, that good shit. I mean, I ain't even had her yet, but I can tell by the way she walk that she got platinum between her thighs."

"Shit. Who you watching that hard?"

"She about thirty-three, got braids in her hair, and got thick thighs and ass. I found out the other day that she can sang 'em under the benches at church and she smart as hell, too. You know her?"

I giggled as my face heated up. "I think I know who you talking 'bout."

"Good. When you see her fine ass, kiss her soft lips for me."

A soft moan escaped me as my eyes closed, imagining one of his soft kisses on my lips. Then my imagination went a step further as I thought about feeling those soft kisses on my lower lips. "I'll do that," I moaned.

"Kendall, you gon' make me have to walk outta here if you keep that up. Can't have everybody in the waiting area seeing me turned on."

"No. All that belongs to me."

"Oh yeah? So you wanna do more than tease it, now?"

I laughed, thinking about our exchanges less than two weeks ago. It seemed like longer than that already. Price stayed on my mind constantly. "Uh huh. I want you to fuck it slow."

"Aww, shit," he said in low voice. "You know the next time I see you, you gon' pay for that, right?"

"I hope so."

"Man, get off my line," he said, then laughed.

I was sitting at my desk feeling so damned horny, I didn't know what to do with myself. "Price, I have to go. The kids are coming back in a few minutes and I have to calm my hot ass down before that."

He laughed more. "I don't know why you wanted to torture us."

I chuckled along with him. That was exactly what I'd done; tortured the hell out of myself. My panties were wet, and it wasn't shit I could do about it. At least I'd be off in less than two hours. I was grateful for my conference period being later in the day. "Okay, Price. I'll call you when I get off work."

"Aight. Get ready to cum when you do."

My eyes closed involuntarily. *Fuck!* My panties felt like I'd already came in them. It was ridiculous. "Price... shit. Okay. Bye."

I hurriedly ended the call, because as long as I was hearing his voice, I wasn't going to be able to gain control of my bodily functions. All I could think about was fucking. It had been years and I was willing to fuck Price anywhere at this point. When the kids walked in, I stood from my chair and cringed at the wetness between my legs. "Ms. Washington, how's Cassie doing? Did you call?"

"Yes, I called. She's doing better. She still hasn't awakened yet, but hopefully that will happen soon."

"You think when she wakes up, you can call her so we can talk to her?"

I swallowed hard, because I wasn't sure what state Cassie would be in when she woke up. She may not be able to talk. Instead of trying to explain that, I said, "Yes."

We continued with the rest of our day and I assigned their home-work and put it in their folders while they completed a science work-sheet. By the time that was done, it was time to go. I realized that my classroom just wasn't the same without Cassie's bright smile. Friday before last, she was like a new kid after I'd combed her hair into a cute bun. I stared at her empty chair until a kid scared the hell out of me. "Ms. Washington, are you okay? You're crying."

I gently pat my face dry. "I'm sorry. Yes, I'm okay. Get in line, sweetie."

I hadn't even realized I was crying. She did as I asked her to, while I gathered my things. "Ms. Washington, were you crying because you're sad about Cassie?"

"I'm okay, y'all. Really. Let's go, so y'all can go home."

I opened the door for them to line up in the hallway, then locked it. My first day back in a week and I have duty. Ugh. I hated it here, in adulthood. I led the kids to the front and sent more than half of them to the cafeteria area to get on their buses, then escorted the other kids to the front to wait on their rides. My phone chimed with a text message, so I took it from my bag to see it was from Price. After unlocking it, I read, *You ready to cum yet?*

He needed something to do. I chuckled as my face heated up. Just a moment ago, I thought I was gonna have to go to the restroom to cry and he'd changed my entire mood that quickly. I responded, *Find you something to do until four-thirty.*

He sent back a laughing emoji, which caused me to smile. Slipping my phone back in my bag, I started helping kids to their rides. A few of the parents of the students in my class had asked about Cassie and said they were still praying for her and that she was on the prayer lists at their churches. Principal Popillion came stood next to me. "How was your first day back?"

"Rough."

"I can imagine. We raised an additional ten-thousand-dollars with our fundraiser this past weekend and the go fund me is at thirty-thousand. Can you believe that? We asked for twenty-thousand, but we've exceeded our goal." She reached in her blazer pocket and gave me an envelope. "Here's the money from the fundraisers."

I accepted the envelope from her and signed a document on her clipboard, stating that I'd received the funds. I opened the envelope to see she'd put the check in Price's name. I'd have to ask him where he banked, so I could deposit it for him. "Thank you. I know I can speak for Price when I say that he undoubtedly needed this, and he appreciates your generosity and love for Cassie."

I hugged her tightly. "Tell him that he's more than welcome. We're family at this school and we take care of each other."

"Yes, ma'am."

"Go ahead and go handle your business. We got this."

"Thank you."

I took off, not wasting a second, so she didn't have time to change her mind. When I got to the car, I called Price. "Damn. You early."

"Shush!" I said while laughing. "I called because I need to deposit a check into your account. Where do you bank?"

"Community Bank. A check from where?"

"The school did two fundraisers and profited $20,113.56."

"Damn! For real?"

"Yes. Everybody loves Cassie and my principal told me to tell you that we're family at Mae Jones-Clark, so we take care of each other."

"Wow. I don't know what to say other than thank you so much."

"I'm on my way to your bank now. I'm gonna try to talk them out of putting a hold on it. Even though it's local, they still might try to put a two-day hold on it."

"They shouldn't. My savings account can cover that check."

I frowned slightly. If he could cover this check, why was he accepting this money? Well, I guess it could go fast if he wasn't working. I quickly checked my judgmental attitude. That was trivial, compared to what he was dealing with. He could very well spend the whole twenty grand before Cassie even got discharged. And who knew how high her deductible could be? "Okay. Hopefully, they don't try to do it anyway. You'll have to give me your account number. I hope you trust me."

"I trust you, Kendall."

Once I got to the bank and was filling out a deposit slip, he gave me his account number. I ended the call with him, so I could handle his business. And just like he'd said, they didn't put a hold on it. Instead, they deposited another grand to it. They'd been keeping up with the news, and realized he was one of their customers. Just that gesture alone had me wanting to move my account there. That's why I liked most local institutions. They seemed to care more about people in the community. The Community Banks in Beaumont were all owned by a local attorney who also owned his own law firm.

When I got back to the car, I noticed without the deposits from the school and the bank, he only had a little over five-hundred-dollars in his checking account. I was assuming he didn't want to touch his savings for whatever reason, but I knew he would have if he had to. I called Price to let him know that I'd deposited it as I headed home. "Hello?"

"Hey. It's done. Your bank also added one thousand to it. They realized you banked with them when it was all over the news."

"Wow. That was extremely nice."

"And I forgot to tell you that the go fund me has thirty grand in it and it's still growing. They had to take the original limit off."

"That's amazing. Whatever I don't use on medical bills and to take care of our basic needs, I'm gonna put in Cassie's savings account."

"That's good, Price."

"So, how was the rest of your day?"

"Miserable without you."

"Same here. Kendall, let me call you back. It's visitation."

"Okay. Talk to you soon."

I ended the call and turned in my driveway. I immediately realized I needed to call the police when I saw that silver Nissan pass by.

CHAPTER 14

P rice

IT HAD BEEN another week and Kendall was back at the hospital
with me. Cassie had been doing well. They planned to wake her up
tomorrow. There was barely any swelling, only broken bones, the
small bleed due to the liver laceration and the head trauma. I was
nervous as to how she would react when she was awake. According to
the scans, she hadn't suffered any brain damage. Although there was
a small bleed when she got here, nothing became of it. I knew I owed
that all to God, because they couldn't explain it.

When Kendall had first gotten here, I'd picked her up and spun
around with her. This past week had been torture without her. Just
sitting up here by myself made the time seem like it was at a stand-
still. While I'd talked to Kendall every day and had even had phone
sex with her late one night, it seemed that only made it move slower. I
was craving her so badly.

I told her that we would go to the hotel room tonight for a while, then come back and wait for the visitation at six tomorrow morning. The last visitation for the night was at ten. She'd stared at me seductively when I'd said so. Since Cassie had been doing well, I'd leave briefly to go take a shower or get something to eat. She was getting further and further out of those woods. The true test would be tomorrow when they woke her up. I was scared and nervous, but excited and anxious all at the same time.

After the last visitation for the night, I told the nurses that I was going to rest and would be back around four the next morning. They assured me that they would call if anything changed. Kendall and I walked hand in hand to the parking garage. She seemed nervous, because there was a slight tremble in her hands. Now wasn't the time to be nervous. She'd been talking big shit over the phone, so it was time to show and prove. I was beyond ready.

The hotel was fifteen minutes away, but it seemed like I had to drive to Beaumont. I was entirely too anxious. "How was the drive, Kendall?"

"It was easy until I got to this Houston traffic. I hate that the most about Houston."

"Yeah, me too. You nervous?"

She smiled slightly. "A little bit."

"You got a lot of shit talking to back up, so I would be nervous too if I were you."

"Price! Really? That only made it worse."

I laughed. "You ain't got nothing to be nervous about. For real. All you gotta do is just be there. I'll handle the rest."

Her face turned red as I rested my hand on her thigh. Damn, I wanted her so bad. I planned to take my time, though. Sleep was something I could get anytime. While she was here, every moment that I wasn't seeing Cassie, I wanted to show her how much I cared and how much I appreciated her for what she'd done for me and Cassie... how much she was still doing for me and Cassie. Not having to touch my savings would be a blessing, until I could get a job again. I still wanted to purchase a house, even though I didn't know what the fate of my relationship with Cassie would be. Like Kendall had said, Cassie was still my daughter regardless of blood, and I was going to fight to the bitter end to keep her.

When we arrived at the hotel, I walked around to the passenger side and opened Kendall's door. The moment she slid out of my truck, I pressed my body against hers and kissed her lips. My hands slowly descended to her ass. I'd been wanting to squeeze that peach for a while now. As I did, Kendall moaned into my mouth, letting me know she was just as ready as I was. Somehow, I managed to pull away from her and close the door, then grabbed her hand. As we walked through the lobby area, I lifted her hand to my lips and kissed it.

After getting on the elevator, I pulled her close once again. She seemed a lot more relaxed and I knew it had to do with that kiss. My need for her wanted me to fuck her right there in the elevator, but I needed her to see that I needed even more than that. Fucking was always good, but I wanted to cherish her body and show her the tenderness, attention, and all that other shit that would turn her ass out.

Once in the room, I smiled at her, then went to the bathroom to start the shower. My dick was already hard just from anticipation. When I went back to the room, Kendall was sitting on the bed and was about to start taking off her clothes. Quickly making my way to her, I grabbed her hands to stop her. "I want tonight to be everything you want it to be. Whatever you desire me to do, I'm gon' do that shit. I want you to know how special you are to me. This isn't just about sex. We've already connected emotionally, mentally, and spiritually. I wanna connect with you physically. I know we haven't been together long, but I feel like you're perfect for me. And not just me, but Cassie, too."

She trembled slightly and I could see the goosebumps on her

flesh. I gently slid my fingertips down her arm, then kissed her bare shoulder. "Kendall, the moment I saw you, my body craved you. So there's no doubt in my mind that you will satisfy me. The way your body reacts to my touch and my voice, I know you'll be satisfied as well."

She remained quiet, but I could tell my words were touching her deep... maybe even touching her soul. I slid her top off her other shoulder and kissed it as well. Slowly pulling her top down her body, I made sure my fingertips slid against her skin as her breathing seemed to shallow. She stepped out of it and I slid my hands up her legs, to the clasp on her pants. It was taking extreme willpower to move as slowly as I was, but I wanted her to the point of desire where she was begging me to fill her.

After I unfastened the clasp on her pants, I slid them down her long, thick ass legs. Once she stepped out of them, I couldn't move. They were so smooth. Starting at the tops of her feet, I blazed a trail of kisses up to her thighs. Before I could stand up, Kendall pulled my shirt over my head. *Fuck!* I wanted to pick her up and just fuck the shit out of her, especially when she slid her palms down my chest after I'd stood. Looking at her in her black strapless bra and matching thong, I couldn't help but lick my lips, then bite the bottom one. She was about to wrap her arms around my neck. "Wait, baby."

"Something wrong?"

"Naw... I just need to admire this beauty before me. Damn..."

My eyes scanned her body, lingering on her cleavage and her thighs, that led to that priceless treasure. Grabbing her hand, I slowly spun her around, rotisserie style, anticipating the juices that would leave that body when I applied some heat to it. Pulling her to me, I stared in her eyes as I unfastened her bra, freeing those beautiful ass breasts. "Oh my God," I said softly.

After rubbing my palms over her erect nipples, I gently toyed with them. Lowering my head, I couldn't help but pull her nipple into my mouth. The gasp that left her had me straining against the zipper of my pants. However, Kendall was ready to remedy that issue. She quickly took off my belt and yanked my pants down. Releasing her nipple, I stood there in my boxer briefs, watching her stare at my erection. That shit was bricked up as if she'd been touching on him or giving me head.

I rested my hands on her hips, then began pulling at the straps of her thong. Going to my knees, I slid them down, revealing her mound as she spread her legs. There was no way that thong was gon' come down them legs if she didn't spread them. I loved her thickness. Looking at her waxed perfection, I put my lips there and kissed it, then quickly stood before I got carried away. She smelled so good. I pulled my drawers down as she seemed to salivate at the sight of it. I grabbed her hand and led her to the shower, so I could prepare that beautiful body for what was to come.

I was trying to take my time, but Kendall was threatening all that shit. She'd gone back to her overnight bag and got her body wash, then began washing my body. When she got to my dick, she started stroking my shit like it was gon' spew black gold. I dropped my head back for a moment and enjoyed her touch and the things it was doing to me. When I knew I was gonna lose control if I let her keep going, I snatched her hand from it and backed her against the wall. I littered her upper body with kisses, then grabbed her loofah and began washing her.

Watching her come fuck me faces were enough to make me do that shit. The way her eyelids fluttered and her lips parted as I touched her, damn near made me cum. But the prize was getting to touch that gem of perfection. As my fingers ran over her lips, she leaned back against the wall, moaning loudly. As I slid past those lips, I knew that she needed my undivided attention there soon.

Once we rinsed off and had gotten out of the shower, we barely pat ourselves dry before I grabbed her hand and brought her to the bed. I laid her on her back then stared at her beautiful temple. God outdid himself when he made her. I slowly shook my head. "You're so beautiful. But I'm about to get you so messy."

I grabbed her by her feet and slowly pulled her to me at the edge of the bed. After kissing her feet, I made my way up her leg, stopping when I got close to the jackpot. I'd hover over it, where she could feel me breathing on it, then start over. Once I'd done both legs a couple of times, I decided to stop teasing her, because she was about to come unglued. She'd thrusted her hips toward my mouth when I got close to it. The juices were leaking from it. She was ripe and ready for me to juice that thang. I slid my fingers between her folds and lightly stroked her clit.

Her body was trembling, and it seemed she was about to go crazy if I didn't do something soon. "Price... please."

"Please what?"

"Stop fucking teasing me. I'm gon' take what I want if you do."

I smiled at her, then bent over and sucked her nipple into my mouth. Using my left hand, I played with her other nipple, and my right hand eased between her legs. I slowly pushed two of my slender fingers inside her as she lifted her hips into them. Stroking her G-spot, I could feel her thighs trembling already. That was okay, though. I'd let her get that first one out. Bringing my mouth to hers, I whispered against her lips, "Give it to me, Kendall."

I rubbed her clit with my thumb and that was all it took. She came all over my fingers. "Price! Shit! Yes!"

It seemed she'd been needing that for a while, but I wasn't done with her. Going to my knees, I stared at her glazed pussy. Her clit was bulging, waiting to meet my tongue, so I didn't make it wait any longer. I flattened my tongue against it and slowly tongue kissed it, making love to it. Tearing my mouth away from her, I had to verbalize what I was feeling. "Shit! You taste good as fuck!"

I quickly went back to it and practically rubbed my whole face in it. *Shit!* I indulged in her taste again... slowly. The way her fruit juiced for me, kept me entranced in her shit. It was like nothing else existed. As I continued to lick and suck on her clit, she started screaming. Kendall grabbed my head and pushed me in further as she came all over my lips. I couldn't stop, though. I was already addicted to her taste. As she tried to get away from me, I wrapped my arms around her thighs and pulled her to me. "Price... babyyyy."

I hummed against her clit, letting her know just how much I already needed her shit. She tried pushing me away, but that shit didn't work either. I journeyed to her ass for a moment, kissing and licking there, too. There wasn't a spot on her body that I wouldn't touch and that was the last place that my lips hadn't been. Those thick thighs started to tremble again, so I stopped. Licking my lips, I stood and went to my duffle bag. I got a few condoms out and threw them to the nightstand, then opened one to strap up.

Once I did, I went back to my knees to get her to the point of no return once again. When she got there, I stopped and slowly pushed my dick inside of her. As I leaned over her, she wrapped her arms around my neck. My eyes closed and I couldn't take the shit. She was so tight. I wanted to make love to her so bad, but my body was saying fuck that. I slid my arms under her legs and yanked her from the bed. Somewhat crashing her body to the wall, I began stroking her, winding that dick inside of her. "Fuck, Kendall!"

My speed quickened as her nails dug into my flesh, wanting me to stop and keep going at the same time. I kissed her lips hungrily as I gripped her ass, pounding into her. "Price! Oh my God!"

"That's it. Call on Jesus. He the only one that can help you. But you don't wanna be helped. You wanna be fucked."

I looked down at how wet my dick was and nearly lost my nut. All that sauce was gon' take me out. Bringing her back to the bed, I pulled out of her and brought my mouth back to her goodness. I couldn't help it. The taste seemed to be fading from my lips, so I had to reup. Kissing her sweetness and slurping up its nectar, I stood and filled her once again. Slowing my pace, I stared into her eyes. "Price, damn. This is everything I thought it would be and more."

I leaned over and kissed her lips, then hooked my arm under her knee and brought it to her shoulder. I began slowly digging for the treasures hidden within her gem. "Price... I'm about to cum again."

"Coat my dick with that shit, then."

I dug deeper as I lifted her other leg to her shoulder. My nut was begging to be set free as well. Her legs trembled and she said, "Here it comes!"

Allowing my nut to come to the surface, I came with her. In that moment, I knew that every free moment I had, I'd be buried deep in her shit.

CHAPTER 15

K endall

IF I HAD to count how many times I came, I wouldn't be able to. Price took care of my body so well last night, I could barely stay awake. Visitation was within another fifteen minutes and I was tired as hell. I laid my head on his shoulder and he put his arm around me and kissed my head. We'd just gotten back to the hospital at five. We'd fucked and made love at least five times. I didn't see how he could stay awake. My body wanted rest, my pussy was throbbing, and my ass felt open. He'd finger fucked my asshole and made that shit nut. *How in the hell did he do that?* I was so sexually overwhelmed, I just wanted to sleep, but he wouldn't let me.

Price had opened my body up and took advantage of every moment my juices leaked. My clit was still tingling, thinking about all the pleasure it received. I nearly fell walking up here. My damn knees buckled when I got off the elevator. Price had to wrap his arm around my waist to help me to a seat. I'd never been so sexually satisfied. If the Lord wanted to take me, he could take me now. Satisfaction didn't even accurately describe what I was feeling. The way he slowly tongue kissed me and my pussy was still on my mind and regardless of how tired I was, my lady parts were still begging for his touch... his kiss... his stroke.

Just as I was about to doze, it was time to go see Cassie. As we stood, Shayla walked in as well, with papers in her hand and a police officer following her. She shot daggers toward us and I didn't have a good feeling about what was about to happen. Price had gotten the abandonment hearing pushed back, due to Cassie being in the hospital. We walked down the hallway in silence as Price glanced at her with a scowl on his face. I immediately started praying, because I was feeling like that police officer was gon' earn every dollar in his salary today.

When we got to Cassie's room, the nurses were all standing there with huge smiles on their faces, blocking the entrance and view inside Cassie's room. We stood there, waiting to see what was going on. As they moved to the side, I could see that Cassie's eyes were open. Price ran inside as the tears fell down my cheeks. "Hey, baby girl! Daddy's here!"

The ventilator was gone, but she still had an oxygen tube in her nose. When I neared her bedside, I heard her whisper, "Daddy..."

She could still talk. I was thanking God for his favor as Price kissed her head. I walked next to him. "Hi, Cassie."

"Ms. Washington," she whispered.

Before we could even get emotionally overwhelmed, Shayla cleared her throat. Cassie's eyes brightened. "Mama!" she whispered excitedly.

She walked over to her bedside and kissed her head. Shayla then looked up at us and said, "So. Since I'm the only biological parent here, I need the two of you to leave. This police officer is here to escort you out and this a restraining order. You are no longer allowed to come here and have to stay at least one hundred feet away from me. And your little assault against me... I'm pressing charges."

The rage that burned within Price was something I'd never seen before. Cassie had begun to cry and I'd joined her. There was nothing we could do. Our hands were tied. Price advanced toward her, but the cop grabbed him. I closed my eyes momentarily and cried aloud as I heard the scuffle that was taking place. *God, please.* When I opened them, I saw the cop putting handcuffs on Price and the tears streaming down my man's face. "I love you, Cassie. I'm gonna find a way to see you, baby. Don't ever forget how much I love you. Okay?"

Through his tears, he glared at Shayla. He communicated with her silently and I could see the terror on her face. "Please get him out of here."

The disgust on the cops face was evident as he pulled Price to the door. "Daddy! Don't leave!" Cassie screamed, her true voice coming through.

As she did, her machines started going crazy. The nurses all came running in and put us all out as Cassie's body seemed to go limp. We weren't even allowed to stay to find out what happened. I began to wale loudly, because I just couldn't take it. Cassie didn't deserve any of this and had we been anywhere else, I would have been catching a charge, too, for fucking Shayla up. Her evilness was beyond me. I couldn't understand why she would take Cassie away from him when she didn't want her just a month and a half ago.

When we got close to the waiting area, the cop stopped and looked at Price. "I'm so sorry. I know this doesn't seem fair to you. When we get to the police station, we'll get your story of how it has come to this. Most likely, you'll be free to go after that. However, the restraining order will still be in place and you won't be allowed to come to the hospital."

"That's my baby. How can I stay away from my baby?"

"According to her, you aren't the biological father."

"Yeah. But we just found that shit out two weeks ago, because Cassie needed blood. She was living with me. Shayla dropped her off at my house for my weekend visit over a month ago and didn't come back. She didn't show up until we were here. I don't even know how she found out what happened."

"Man," the cop said as he ran his hand down his face.

"Yeah, I assaulted her. But it was in that moment when the doctor told me that the child I've been taking care of for eight years... the angel that I loved more than myself... wasn't mine. I grabbed her by the neck. But she wasn't hurt. She didn't need medical attention. In fact, they felt so sorry for me, they didn't even call y'all. I hate that bitch."

I wanted to tell Price to stop talking, but I didn't want it to seem like he had anything to hide, because he didn't. I leaned against the wall, the tears still falling from my eyes. Walking over to Price, I hugged him tightly. "Can I follow you to the police station?" I asked the cop once I let Price go.

"Yes ma'am."

I exhaled loudly as Price looked in the direction of Cassie's room. His eyes were red along with his skin. I knew if they wouldn't have cuffed him, she would have had a reason to file assault charges. While I didn't condone him hitting a woman, I would have turned my head the other direction while he fucked Shayla up. I wanted to fuck her up myself, but I knew we had to play this smart if we ever wanted to see Cassie again. One of Cassie's nurses came out of the ICU wing and I ran to her. "Please tell me Cassie is okay."

"Yes, ma'am. She's okay. Just the circumstances over excited her and caused a lack of oxygen to her brain, which caused her to pass out. I was hoping we wouldn't have to hook her back up to the ventilator, because she was doing so well without it. I'm so sorry about what has happened. After this, I can't give you anymore information on the patient."

She exhaled loudly as I cried aloud once again. I nodded my head and walked over to Price. "Cassie is okay. She'd just passed out."

Price didn't say a word as the cop led us out of the hospital. He agreed to wait for me at the hospital's entrance. As I walked to the parking garage, I couldn't believe what had happened. The law was so fucking black and white and the people that were in the gray area were just assed out. Price was assed out and he may never get to see Cassie again. I didn't know how he would make it without Cassie, but I prayed for God to give me strength to be there for him.

WHEN WE GOT BACK to the hotel room, Price looked so defeated. He'd told the detective everything, starting from when Shayla dropped Cassie to him. The disgust everyone felt was evident in their facial expressions. Price hadn't said a word since we'd left the police station and I didn't know what to do to make him feel any better. I felt helpless and not only that, but I didn't really feel like talking either. I was hurt, so I knew he was dying inside. After getting inside our room, he fell in the bed face first.

I got in with him and gently rubbed his back and the back of his head. Price looked up at me with tears in his eyes, then pulled me to him. He wrapped his arms around me as he laid on my chest. "What am I supposed to do now?"

"I don't know, baby. I wish I did."

"She's my world, Kendall. I'm just supposed to forget about her? Pretend that she never existed? Shayla gon' suffer for this shit."

"Well, listen. While we think this over and how we can proceed, I want you to stay with me. Okay?"

He looked up at me again, then kissed me softly. "Or you can stay with me."

"Whatever we decide, I don't want you to be alone more than what you have to be."

"I don't want to be. Not right now anyway. 'Cause I'm tempted to drive up to that hospital and do some serious damage."

"That was so painful. It still is. I'd only gotten a month with her." I exhaled as Price laid back on my chest. "What if we can prove that she's unfit?"

"Then CPS would take her. I'm not her father, remember?"

"Shit." I scratched my head. My head always itched when I got worked up. "CPS is always looking to place kids somewhere, though. You might have to get certified to be a foster parent, but you also have proof that she's lived with you before. The school records only have your name and your brother's name on it."

Price didn't say anything in response. I assumed he just wanted to drop it for now. I rubbed his head and started humming "The Battle Is the Lord's" by Yolanda Adams. He hugged me tighter and I could feel moisture from his tears on my chest. I used to sing in church all the time and outside of church, only people close to me knew that. Rubbing the back of his head, my mission was to help ease his pain and relax him. The more I hummed and rubbed his head, the heavier he got on my chest.

When I looked down at him, he was asleep. I continued rubbing the back of his head and humming, feeling defeated. There had to be a way out of this. The only problem was that all the solutions I came up with, Shayla still held the power. So, my prayer now was that the Lord would soften her heart. Cassie was gonna be miserable without Price and I prayed that her emotional state didn't worsen her condition. Shayla was a miserable bitch. I laid there humming and thinking and then a light bulb came on. That bitch was after that money. If Price didn't have Cassie and wasn't coming to see her and missing work, he would have to turn it over to Cassie's guardian.

I peeped game and that bitch had better watch her back. I'd make sure she couldn't touch any of that money. My principal could make sure that money went into a trust fund for Cassie. I was more than sure that the donors wouldn't have a problem with that. Price began to snore lightly, and I was grateful he was getting rest. He hadn't slept. Neither had I, so I was about to join him until my phone rang. Fishing through my purse next to me with one hand, I silenced it, then answered the random number. "Hello?"

"Hi, Kendall. I just wanted to see how you were doing."

"Got damn, nigga! Are you slow? You have to be, because I done told yo' ass several times to stop calling me. I've blocked every number you've called from and you still find a way to get to me. Why?"

Price sat up and looked at me and I immediately regretted answering the phone. "Because I'm feeling you Kendall. It's been a while since I felt connected to any woman the way I feel for you. I can't let that go. Why can't you see that you're supposed to be with me?"

Price snatched the phone from me. "Yo. She said don't call her no more. I'm on some 'I ain't got shit to lose' shit. I will find you and come fuck you up. That's on my life. Now, if you can't respect her, you gon' respect these hands I got for you. And if that ain't enough, I got something even deadlier for you. Now quit fucking calling her."

He ended the call, then stared in my eyes. I was somewhat nervous, because I didn't know what he was thinking. He grabbed one of my braids and twirled it between his fingers. My breathing pattern had changed, and I believed he noticed. He looked down at my chest, then back into my eyes. "He a fuck up. I'm gon' show him how much of one he is. Let me know if he keeps calling you."

"Price, it isn't that serious. I'll change my number."

"Did you sleep with him?"

I frowned slightly. Why was that any of his business if I did? As if reading my mind, he said, "That would explain his infatuation. That's why I'm asking. This nigga giving me fatal attraction vibes and shit."

"No. We didn't sleep together, and we only kissed once. It wasn't an involved kiss like you and I have. It was maybe three seconds... if that. Truthfully, I felt like I only used him to keep my attention away from you."

Price's hand slid down my body, lingering on my breast. "Well, I'm glad that façade didn't last. I told you that you belong to me. Now that I done got to taste you, that's a wrap. Call me what you want and you can feel however you want to feel about it, but you ain't going nowhere."

He laid back on my chest, not giving me a chance to respond. I knew what he said had a lot to do with what happened today. If he lost me while the wound was still open from losing Cassie, then he would lose it. To bring the subject back to her instead of me, I said, "I think Shayla's after money."

"I ain't got no money, so that bitch barking up the wrong tree."

"Yes, you do. You have fifty grand. The go fund me is public, so she knows about thirty of it for sure."

"You know, you shol' in the fuck right. I ain't even got the thirty grand yet, though."

"I know. So, I can possibly request that it be put into a trust fund for Cassie. You wanna do that?"

"Yeah. Monday, ask your principal if she can do that. But she could still get to it right?"

"Well, some banks require that you let it sit for a certain amount of time. It's worth a try."

"Yeah. Damn, I miss my baby."

"I know. I miss her, too." I pulled him back to my chest. "Maybe in an hour or so, you wanna try to get lunch?"

"I know you're probably hungry, but I don't have much of an appetite."

"You think maybe if you ride out with me, you'll change your mind?"

"Maybe. I'm hoping that they'll call me to come see Cassie. I was thinking about checking out today, but I don't wanna give up so easily."

"I understand. Why don't you wait until tomorrow to check out? Today has been rough enough without you having to drive home. Just chill out today and try to rest."

I kicked off my shoes and got all the way in the bed, laying my head on the pillow. Price kicked off his shoes as well and took off his shirt, then pulled the covers up and over us. He laid his body partially on mine and again wrapped his arms around my waist and laid his head on my shoulder and chest. This time, after kissing his head, then his lips, I fell asleep with him.

CHAPTER 16

P rice

I KNEW what hell felt like. Staying at Kendall's house for the past week, I still hadn't heard from the doctors. I tried calling once, but they wouldn't give me any information. I was so pissed... hurt... defeated... dismayed. Depression was consuming me, so I called my job to see if they'd hired anyone in my position yet and they hadn't. When I told my dispatcher what had gone down, she started crying. Thankfully, they didn't put in my resignation, so it was like I just had time off. I needed something to do to keep my mind busy.

Kendall had been amazing. She'd been taking care of me emotionally and mentally. She'd been down too, so I decided that I would cook for her. I came to my apartment to wash clothes and straighten up since my load canceled for the day. Kendall was still at work. I was so grateful for her, because I didn't know where I would be without her support. While I had my brother, he had a family to be concerned with, along with a full-time job. Karter was pissed when I told him what had happened, and Tricia cried. Cassie had buried herself deeply in everyone's heart she'd come in contact with.

When we first got back, Kendall's family had come over to her house with food. Just their company was uplifting and keeping my mind off the nightmare I was living. They'd promise to come back this coming weekend and my brother and his family were planning to come over as well. After I'd put clothes up and packed a fresh bag, I went back to Kendall's. Next week, I was going to go back to my place. I was hoping she didn't take that the wrong way, but I didn't want to live on her. That didn't even feel right to me as a man. She wouldn't let me pay for anything. I wasn't a weak nigga that couldn't take care of himself.

While I still missed Cassie, I wasn't feeling as bad as I did a week ago. I had no clue how she was doing or progressing, though, and that was hard as hell. All I could do was pray that she was doing well, and that I'd eventually get to see her. When I got inside, I took out her pressure cooker and put on some red beans with sliced sausage in it, then poured oil in a pan to fry the chicken. Kendall would be home in an hour, and I wanted her to be surprised. While the chicken was frying, I put the flowers on the table and made sure the wine she liked was chilling in the fridge.

After everything was in place, I heard Kendall speed in the driveway and come to a screeching stop. I didn't know what was going on. I'd put my truck in the garage, so she wouldn't know I was here. I watched her from the window, run inside the house. *What the fuck was up?* There was another car in the driveway. I went to the door only for her to run into me and start screaming. I held her to me. "What's going on?"

"He's following me."

Right after she said that, that muthafucka was at the back door. When he saw me, he started backing his ass up. "Naw. What the fuck I told you last time over the phone?" I could see Kendall in my peripheral, calling someone, probably the police. "I'm 'bout to fuck you up."

I charged towards his ass, knocking him to the ground. We tussled for a minute and he gut checked me as I laid one across his jaw. I rolled off him but stood before he could pounce on me. He came at me, but his pursuit came to a screeching halt when I kicked him in his stomach. Then I had my way with his bitch ass. I'd knocked him out. Then I saw smoke. *Shit!* I was frying chicken. The police drove in the driveway as I ran inside to get the skillet off the fire. My damn chicken was black. I didn't know which way Kendall had gone. I was careful when I walked back toward the door. West's ass was still out, but I didn't want the police to think I was the perp.

"Freeze!"

I raised my hands and stood still as I saw Kendall coming from the front room. She looked scared. I didn't know what all had happened, but I was sure I was about to find out. "He's not the perp. The one on the ground is," she said softly.

The officer lowered his weapon as Kendall fell into my arms. Wrapping my arms around her, I said, "It's okay, baby."

"Price, he was at my job, waiting for me in the parking lot and I barely got away from him."

"Tell the police what happened, baby."

I noticed that the other cop was helping him to his feet, then handcuffed him. "He'd been blowing my phone up from an unknown number all day. My phone won't block an unknown number. I should've called the cops then, but I thought he was harmless. Maybe a little mentally slow, but that was it. When I got off and was walking to my car, he was standing next to it. I started screaming at him and he grabbed me by the arm, telling me he just needed to talk to me. One of my coworkers saw him and yelled. When he released me, I hopped in my car and took off. He followed me here."

I'd heard enough as the cop asked how they knew one another. As I was about to walk to the door, Kendall quickly latched on to my arm. "Please don't leave me, Price."

"It's okay, baby. I won't leave."

I sat down next to her and listened to the details of their relationship. I found myself rolling my eyes a couple of times and tuning the conversation out completely. When I did, my mind went to Cassie. I was wondering what she was doing and how she was handling not seeing me. Keeping myself busy had been helping, but whenever I had a moment to myself, thoughts of her made my heart heavy. I didn't know how I was going to see her again, but I had to somehow.

Once the police were done with their report and filing a restraining order against West, a wrecker came and got his car. Kendall was clinging to me. I was glad it was Friday, so she didn't have to go anywhere tomorrow. "I'm sorry I burned dinner. I was trying to surprise you."

"I'm sorry. I should've been paying closer attention. I was just trying to get away from him. Thank you for having my back."

"Kendall, you're my woman. I'll always have your back, just like you have mine." I kissed her head. "Come on. Let's clean this mess in the kitchen, then we'll have to get something to eat."

It smelled a horrible mess in the house. We cleaned up as quickly as possible. I hated that dinner was ruined, but there would be other times. When we were done, we got cleaned up and headed to Chili's.

LAST NIGHT WAS ROUGH. After we'd gotten back from dinner and had gone to bed, Kendall tossed and turned all night. With yesterday's events, I knew I wouldn't be going home, so I didn't bother bringing it up. Leaving her, with the way she was, would be cruel. She needed me. However, at about four, she finally started sleeping soundly. I took that opportunity to get some sleep as well.

By the time I woke up, it was ten and Kendall was still asleep, mouth wide open. I chuckled, then I quickly got up to get ready for everyone that was coming today. Both our families would be here to keep us company and cook. They knew how hard a time we were having not being able to be there for Cassie. I would have never thought Shayla would do some shit like this. She knew taking Cassie from me would break me. The killing thing was that she was acting like I was the one that had done something wrong.

I'd grabbed her by her damn neck in response to knowing that she'd deceived me for nine years. When she told me she was pregnant, she knew it wasn't for me. Even if she didn't know for sure, she should have been honest about that shit and said that it was possible Cassie was for someone else. To have her in my life, then suddenly removed from it without warning, was cruel as fuck. Cassie was probably for that nigga she was fucking around with before me. There was no way for me to know, though, because Cassie looked just like her, and we'd been together for almost two years when she got pregnant.

She was the one that had fucked me over. Took my money for years for a child that wasn't mine. If she was after money like Kendall seemed to think, I was gon' hang her ass in court. There were still the abandonment charges that we had to go to court for. I wondered if that even mattered now. At the time, I was under the impression that I was Cassie's daddy. She was awake and was able to speak. It was a miracle that I barely got to witness. The pain on my baby's face when she screamed made things so much worse for me.

As I made my way to the front, I saw Kendall's parents coming to the back door. I opened it before they could ring the doorbell or knock. Kendall needed her rest. When they came in, Mrs. Washington hugged me, and Mr. Washington shook my hand. Alana and P were right behind them carrying bags. I was sure it was food to cook. Once they sat them on the countertops, they both hugged me, then went to the couch. "How are you and Kendall?" P asked.

I shrugged my shoulders. "We're good. She didn't sleep well last night. That punk had my baby having nightmares."

"Yeah. I heard you took care of him real good," Alana said and chuckled.

"Hell yeah. He thought she was alone. You should've seen his face when he saw me. Ain't no way he was gon' make it out of here without proof that he'd come in contact with me."

"See, P. That's gon' be bruh-in-law. I'm telling you."

I did my best to hold in my smile, then said, "We ain't even in love yet and you planning a wedding."

"Man, tell that to somebody that ain't seen the way y'all look at each other. Kendall ain't never let nobody stay in her house. She not only have you staying here, but she letting you stay here when she ain't here. That shit speaks volumes."

"Maybe so, but until she says it, we gon' take it one day at a time."

"Uh huh."

Alana sat back and crossed her legs as I noticed my baby coming down the hallway. I stood and walked over to her. She wrapped her arms around my neck and kissed my lips. "Good morning, baby. How long has everyone been here?"

"Good morning. They just got here a few minutes ago. Did you rest well this morning?"

"Yeah, I did. Thank you."

"Listen. You don't have to thank me every time I do something for you or show concern. You belong to me, right?"

"Yeah. Only you. And you belong to me."

"Aight, then. It's only right to check on my possessions and baby, you a prize."

She lowered her head as a smile graced her lips. When she looked up again, her cheeks were rosy. Grabbing her hand, I led her to the kitchen to speak to her parents. They were making gumbo. I could go for that shit, on the real. My stomach was growling already. She hugged the both of them, then went and sat next to her crazy ass sister. When she sat, she hugged her tightly. "That fool had the wrong one yesterday, huh?"

"Yeah," Kendall said, glancing at me.

The doorbell rang, so I knew it was my brother and his family. I opened the door and welcomed them inside. They all spoke to everyone, since they'd met them last weekend. Tricia was heading to the kitchen. Everyone got alarmed. Once she kissed Kendall's parents, Karter gently pulled her out the kitchen to the front room where we were. All of us were trying to hide our snickers. Tricia still hadn't mastered cooking. I mean she was probably a great cook for a white family, but she hadn't tried to change it up at all for her black family. So, whenever she headed to the kitchen when other people were cooking, Karter always pulled her out of it. They'd been married for twelve years and she still hadn't learned.

They sat on the other couch, across from me and Kendall. We were seated in the oversized chair together. As Tricia and P talked Karter and Alana talked as well. Their son and daughter had gone to the extra bedroom to watch TV. Kendall had shown them where it was the last time they were here. Kendall sunk down in the corner of the chair and I pulled her legs to my lap. Gently rubbing them up and down with one hand, I grabbed her hand with the other and kissed it. "Y'all are so cute."

I looked up to see Alana making googly eyes at us. Slightly rolling my eyes, she laughed. Although I'd only met her for the first-time last week at the hospital, it seemed like I'd known her forever. Last weekend, we'd talked about Kendall a lot. Kendall was the total opposite of everything she told me she was. That was why she was already planning the wedding. With me, Kendall was so soft, somewhat timid, and kind. The only thing we both agreed on was that she was nasty.

Kendall rolled her eyes as well, then slid her hand down the side of my face and smiled. I noticed Tricia getting up and we all watched her until Karter said, "Oh, she's just going to the bathroom."

When she was out of ear shot, we all laughed, including Karter. Shortly after, Tricia's phone chimed on the coffee table where she'd left it. No one really payed attention to it once we realized it was her phone. But then, it chimed back to back like four or five times. Karter picked it up. "You have the code to her phone?" Alana asked.

"Uh... yeah. That's my wife. Why wouldn't I?"

She shrugged her shoulders as Karter unlocked Tricia's phone. Call us nosy, but we were all watching him to see why her phone was chiming so much. Karter's face had turned completely red. That wasn't a hard feat to accomplish, being that he was high-yellow. "Bruh, let me talk to you outside."

"Aight."

I kissed Kendall as I stood from my seat and followed him out the back door. "What's up?"

He shoved the phone into my chest, and I looked at it to see text messages from Shayla. *What the fuck?* As I read over the messages, I could see that Tricia was telling Shayla that I didn't know how to take care of a little girl and that she needed to come back for Cassie. Then she told her that it was my fault Cassie got hit by a truck, because I didn't pay close enough attention to her. I was fuming. I wanted to go in that house and snatch her ass bald. However, when I looked at the last text messages, Shayla was complaining about how she couldn't do this.

Cassie had been crying and begging for me since I'd left. When I saw the words, *him and his bitch,* I almost lost it. Shayla went on to say that she hated staying at the hospital all day. Tricia's message had said, *But it will be all worth it when you get all that money they raised.* All this shit was Tricia's idea. I wondered how much of a kickback she was getting for feeding Shayla information. Shayla's final set of messages said, *I'm gonna call Price.*

I can't do this.

This lil girl is driving me insane.

As I was holding the phone, Tricia responded from her watch. *You forgot that he knows Cassie isn't his?*

She couldn't be that damn stupid. Tricia had to know that Karter had picked her phone up by now. Her message had also semi-confirmed that Shayla knew that Cassie wasn't mine. I looked up at him and handed him the phone back. He started pacing. "Bruh, I wanna hurt her. I'm so sorry."

"It's okay. That's not on you."

The best part was that Shayla was planning to call me. Cassie may be in my life again after all. While I was pissed that Tricia had caused all this fuck shit, I couldn't help but be happy that I was gonna get to have Cassie back. Tricia flew out the back door as me and Karter stood there staring at her. Her eyes traveled to the phone in Karter's hands. "Karter, I can explain."

"The fuck you will. Let's go."

I had somewhat of a smirk on my face, but I wasn't enthused. I wanted to choke her ass with her own hair. "What about the kids?"

"Bruh, can they stay here until I come back to get them?"

"Yeah. That's cool, bruh."

He grabbed her by the arm, and they walked to the car. I watched them until she jerked away from him. Hopefully, he didn't do anything that would land him in jail. I walked back in the house and Kendall, Alana, and P were all staring at me, waiting for me to fill them in. Mr. and Mrs. Washington were watching TV. "Tricia has been talking to Shayla and directing her on what she should do about Cassie."

Kendall covered her mouth with her hand as Alana stood from her seat. "Where she at?"

"They left. Believe me, Karter is gonna handle this. I just hope I don't have to bail him out of jail later. He was so pissed. But the good news is that Shayla is having a fucking meltdown being stuck in that hospital. She wants to give Cassie back to me. I'm just waiting on her phone call, so I can make a fucking beeline to Texas Children's."

Kendall, Alana, and P all started dancing and hopping around the front room as I laughed. "Yo, y'all calm down. While I'm happy, I don't wanna get my hopes up. Tricia was trying to talk Shayla out of calling me. Like you said, baby, it's about the money. So, I'm glad we did what you suggested."

"Me too."

Kendall hugged me tightly as I thanked God for that silver lining.

CHAPTER 17

K endall

IF I HAD to thank God for one person or thing, right now that would be Price Daniels. He'd been there for me endlessly this week. I took off work that Monday, but I'd gone all the other days. West hadn't tried to call me, and I hadn't noticed anyone following me, so I hoped he got the message this time. I didn't even know that Price was home, but I was extremely grateful that he was. Surprisingly, he didn't question me about reporting a car following me to the police the week before and not telling him about it. He'd zoned out a couple of times while I was talking, though, so that was probably why he'd missed that.

After that day, I did some checking on West McFall and found out that he'd gotten fired from the fire department a couple of years ago, which was why he had so much time on his hands to follow me every damn where. He'd also been arrested for something like this a year ago. I wasn't worried about his ass until he grabbed me. That was when I got scared.

I'd been in a relationship where things had threatened to get ugly. My boyfriend at the time had a horrible temper. The nigga got angry about something. I didn't even remember what he'd gotten angry about, but he grabbed me and shook me real good. After that, I left his ass and pressed charges. So, when West grabbed me, I knew I had to get away from his ass, because at that point, I didn't know what he was capable of.

The way Price fucked this dude up, I knew I had the right man on my team. After I got over being scared, I was horny as hell. However, he didn't try to make love. We actually hadn't had sex since we left Houston. We'd been so worried about Cassie and we still were. It had been a week and there still hadn't been any word. Price tried calling Shayla, but she must have had his number blocked. We were hoping that she would reach out this weekend. I really hoped she did, because it was like Price had gotten his hopes up only to be let down.

When I walked in the door from work, I started on dinner. Price was still at work, but he would be here shortly. I had after school duty, so I didn't get home until almost five. It was crazy how some parents didn't show up to get their kids until after four. School let out at three-thirty. I understood some of them didn't get off work until four, but damn. There were a significant number of kids that were still there. I would never believe that all of them were at work. Days in the classroom had gotten easier, but I still stared at Cassie's seat during my conference period.

After sliding the enchiladas in the oven, I sat on the couch to watch TV, anticipating Price's arrival. Not only did I want to cater to him, but I wanted to fuck him senseless. Help ease his mind if only for a little while. The situation with West had given him more to worry about and I knew he was wound tight. After he'd fucked me and made love to me in that hotel room two weeks ago, it was all I could think about. Being with Price was something I'd craved from the moment I met him. Now that I was with him, I couldn't get enough of him. Not just sexually, but mentally, emotionally, spiritually.

Every free moment I had, I was calling him to see what he was doing and how his day was going. Most times, he was either driving or waiting to be loaded or unloaded, but he said he loved when I called him. He said it made his day go by faster. Being in his arms when he got home in the evenings was the intimacy I'd been craving and it seemed he craved that, too. The entire time he held me, he would place soft kisses on my head and anywhere else his lips could easily access.

Standing from the sofa, I made my way to the kitchen to get the enchiladas from the oven when the doorbell rang. I frowned slightly, because no one ever just popped up at my house. They always called first. I hesitantly walked to the door and saw Shayla through the glass. *What in the fuck was she doing here?* When I saw her, I ran to the door. I thought something had happened to Cassie. Because she was a minor, an adult was supposed to be with her when possible, especially during these hours. Late night hours, they weren't as strict about it for ICU patients. I swung the door open and stared at her. "I know I was the last person you were expecting to see at the door."

Damn right. I didn't respond verbally, just stared at her. She fidgeted a bit, but it became worse when Price drove in the driveway. "Cassie isn't doing too well. She wants her daddy and I'm tired of trying to convince her that I love her, too. She had to be sedated once y'all left, because she screamed and cried so much. I know y'all probably hate me and I'm sorry. But she needs him."

Price walked towards the back door with a scowl on his face, but it quickly disappeared, as if he thought of the reason she could have been here. When he got closer, she cowered some and took a step back, closer to me. "Why are you here, Shayla? How is Cassie?"

"She misses her daddy and Ms. Washington. I'm sorry. I dropped the assault charges and the restraining order. Just go back to her."

"Why? This ain't a setup is it?"

"No. She needs you. She isn't progressing anymore without you. She's refusing to talk anymore and is just sleeping a lot. I don't want to see her die. While I'm not the best person to take care of her, I do love her. Cassie loves you so much, it seems like she'd rather die than be without you. She has no more fight in her. I'm gonna go back tonight, but if you can come tomorrow, it will help her tremendously. I know it will."

"How did you know where Kendall lived?"

"Tricia."

He glanced over at me, then said, "We'll be there first thing in the morning."

While I hated what she'd done to Price, I was so happy that she had a change of heart. Before I could stop myself, I grabbed her and pulled her into a tight hug, probably cutting off her circulation. I was so happy, I couldn't contain it. Shockingly, she hugged me, too. When I let her go, I said, "I'm sorry. I couldn't contain my excitement. We miss Cassie so much and I have been so depressed. Not knowing how she was doing was killing us."

Price smiled softly at me as Shayla nodded her head and turned to leave. "Thanks, Price, for being an amazing dad to Cassie."

He nodded his head at her, then we both watched her walk to her car. Price put his arm around me, and once Shayla was gone, he smiled brightly. "I have my daughter back!"

He lifted me in his arms as I giggled. "Come on. Let's eat, so we can pack."

"What are we eating," he asked as we walked inside.

"Enchiladas with Spanish rice and beans."

He wrapped his arms around my waist from behind, halting my progress. Pulling me into him, he dipped his head to my ear. "What's for dessert?"

My breathing quickened. "Whatever you want, Price."

"What if I said I wanted that pussy for dessert?"

I damn near came on myself just from his words. "What if I said you can have that as an appetizer, the main course and dessert? I'll strip right here and lay on the dinner table."

"Don't tempt me, girl. I'll fuck you up, I'm so got damned happy. My soul is relieved and I wanna show you what that shit feel like."

"Well, fuck. Let me get the enchiladas from the oven, before they burn, and you can have all this shit."

He slapped my ass as I walked away. His voice and the fact that he wanted me as badly as I wanted him, had my panties overflowing. Once I pulled the enchiladas from the oven, I said, "Here, come eat. Then we'll shower and I can indulge in you for hours."

"Hours, huh? You gon' tap out long before that. I'm gon' eat and suck on that pussy so good, that body gon' go into convulsions."

I glanced back at him as I fixed his plate and his stare made me gush even more. He wasn't playing and I needed some of that action ASAP. He was so damn sexy. When I finally found my words, I said, "Well, after the convulsions, I'm gon' fuck some shit up, too. Don't count me out so easily."

"Well, shit, let me hurry up and eat," he said as I sat his plate in front of him.

After fixing my plate and getting us drinks, I sat next to him. Grabbing my hand, he proceeded to bless our food. When he was done, we dug in. Not many words were needed after that. Price groaned as he ate, voicing his complete satisfaction with the food. I was happy he liked it, because I planned to cater to him for the rest of my life. I could never leave him. We'd never really argued. That moment about West wasn't really an argument. I was the only one talking, trying to explain myself. "This is so good, Kendall. I can't wait until I can properly thank you."

"How will you properly thank me?"

"Oh, I guess you need a preview."

He yanked my chair to him and wrapped his arms around me tightly, then laid his mouth on mine, causing my internal organs to quake, registering an eight point nine on the Richter scale. When he eased away from me, he gently pulled my bottom lip with his teeth.

My mind was screaming, *fuck that food!* "You think you can take some more of that?"

"Mmm hmm," I said softly, my eyes still closed.

When I opened them, Price was staring at me like he wanted to lay me on this table. He wouldn't get any objections from me. I stared right back, my mouth slightly open and my eyes low, letting him see how turned on I was, Price had me like a fucking Little Caesar's pizza; hot and ready. Grabbing his fork, he scooped some food from his plate, and fed me. Our eyes locked in and this shit was so sensual, I couldn't help but stand to my feet and straddle him. Price licked his lips and let his hand travel to my ass. When he squeezed, my eyes closed, enjoying the feeling. He began tugging at my shirt and pulled my breast from my bra, then swirled his tongue around my nipple. My hands traveled to the back of his head holding him there. A slight moan left my lips, then he closed his mouth around it and began gently sucking. I unfastened my bra and gave him full access.

Price moaned as he continued sucking my nipple, then reached up and toyed with the other with his fingertips. His hands then slid their way into my pants and grabbed my bare ass. "Price, what about dinner?"

"That's what they make microwaves and ovens for. This shit right here can't wait."

I couldn't help but moan in response as he gripped my ass even tighter. Resting my arms on his shoulders and clasping my hands by intertwining my fingers, I lowered my head to his shoulder and rested it there. My hips began grinding on his erection that was evident through his pants, not to mention how I felt it between my legs. It was a slow grind that had my clit protruding, rubbing against the seat of my panties. "Mmm, Price."

"What's up, baby?" he asked as he lifted his hips.

"Why you turn me on so much?"

"Because you the one for me and I'm the one for you." He lifted his hips into me, teasing me like I was teasing him. "You know why else?"

He kissed my neck and gently sucked my skin, right beneath my earlobe, causing me to release a moan. Price knew I liked that shit. "Why?" I moaned breathlessly.

"Because you're in love with me."

My eyes opened slowly, and I stared into his. My fucking tongue was frozen like a block of ice. I couldn't speak. *Was I in love with him already?* My hips maintained their rhythm as if he didn't just drop a bomb on my ass. As I opened my mouth to say something, he put his fingers on my lips. "Shh. Think about it. Don't confirm or deny."

I gently pulled one of his fingers into my mouth and sucked on it like it was a dick. When he withdrew it from my mouth, he pulled his shirt off. I loved his chest. Dragging my nails down his tatts, to his nipples, his head dropped back. His nipples were extremely sensitive. I'd learned that the last time we had sex. I flicked them gently with my nails and it was like his dick got harder. Price grabbed my hands, then stood while still holding me and went to my bedroom.

I was starting to feel a lil sensitive, realizing this would be our last night sleeping together for a long while. When we left to get to Cassie tomorrow, I knew I would be alone in my house for a long time. I knew he really didn't like being here. Price was a proud man and he wanted to be in charge of things. He'd put his feelings to the side for me, especially after what happened with West. I would be back to seeing him on the weekends, so I knew we had to make the most out of tonight.

Price sat me on the bed, then went to the bathroom to start the shower. As I sat there, I could feel my emotions getting the best of me. I *did* love him. Price had gotten what no man had ever gotten from me; all of me. He had my heart, my soul, my mind, and I willingly gave it all to him without a fight. In a short amount of time, I would do anything for him and Cassie. When he came back to the room, he grabbed my hands and pulled me to a standing position. It was like I was in a trance, staring at his sexy ass. He'd completely disrobed while he was in the bathroom and it seemed as if I couldn't do a damn thing for myself. Tearing my eyes away from his, I began pulling at my pants. Price rested his hands atop mine, halting my progress. "Naw. I got this, baby."

After I'd looked up at him, I once again averted my gaze and I tried to focus on my feet. I'd allowed myself to get overwhelmed, and it felt like I was about to cry. This shit was unreal. I was feeling what Jill Scott was talking about in "He Loves Me." He'd ignited a fire in me that couldn't be smothered by anyone, not even me. Whenever I saw him, it was like my body said, *come and get me.* Even the first day I saw him, my body was tingling all over. Resting my hands on his shoulders, I lifted my legs one at a time out of my pants.

When he stood, he laid his lips on mine. His kiss caused the tears to fall from my eyes, ripping me of all restraint. It was like he was my drug and I'd been fiending for another dose. I was an addict of his love, his touch, and just his presence. He led me to the shower and once we were in the bathroom, he turned to look at me. My tears must have stained my cheeks, because he gently rubbed his thumb across my cheek. "You okay?"

I nodded my head, then sat on the countertop. Pulling my knees to my chest, I saw his dick hop in anticipation. Price came to me slowly and slid his fingers inside of me. The pleasure was immeasurable, and I knew when he slid his dick inside of me, I would cum immediately. He leaned over my body, causing me to lean back as he rested his hand on the mirror behind me. In two swift motions, he took his fingers out of me and pushed his dick inside. My lashes fluttered as I leaned back on my elbows. Price put his fingers in his mouth and sucked my juices from them.

He then leaned in and kissed my lips, giving me his tongue. Pulling away from me, he hooked my leg with his arm and brought it to my shoulder as he stroked me slowly. That shit pulled the rest of the tears I'd put a lock on right out of me. "This what you needed baby?"

"Hell yeah."

He was going excruciatingly slow, and I didn't know how he could handle it. My pussy was trying to suck him in. His stare was on me and I did my best to avoid that shit. I was about to cum and he hadn't hardly done shit yet. He allowed his dick to fall out of me, then put it right back in. "Oh, fuck! Price!"

Right after that, he plunged into me, nearly taking my breath away. It was like his damn hips were on a swivel. The way those circular motions were fucking with my G-spot, I wanted to slap the shit out of him and tell him I loved him at the same time. My entire body started to tremble, and I came all over him. "Oh, this how you feeling, baby? You gon' cum a lot tonight. You know why?"

"Why?"

"Because I need to show you how much I love you. I need to worship this body for the perfection that it is and tell it how much I appreciate it for housing this heart of gold. Everything about you is perfect, Kendall. I love you."

I couldn't contain my emotions and I cried like a baby all while still trying to throw my hips at him. He started to really fuck me up as he placed his hand on my neck, slightly choking me. I again came all over him. I'd never cum back to back like that. The way his dick was fucking me, had my body tripping, doing shit it didn't normally do. As I came down from my orgasm, I stared in his eyes. "I love you, too, Price."

He frowned slightly and slammed his hand into the mirror, then pulled his dick out of me and shot nut all over my stomach. "Fuck!"

My admission must have gotten him there quicker than he wanted. His skin was red as hell, but when he looked into my eyes, his entire body seemed to relax. Scooping me from the countertop, he brought me to the shower. I could barely stand after those two orgasms, but somehow, I accomplished the feat. "I'm sorry, baby."

I lifted my hands to his face as he continued to stare at me. "What are you sorry for?"

"I didn't ask if it was okay for me to go in raw. I was so caught up with the beautiful sight before me. Your pussy is beautiful, and that shit was leaking that goodness. A condom was the last thing on my mind."

I released the breath I was holding. I was hoping he didn't have bad news. Pulling his face to mine, I communicated how I didn't give a fuck about that by kissing him. Practically putting my tongue down his throat, he got the point. Before my entire body could get wet from the shower spray, he was lifting me against the wall and filling me once again. He was extremely red again and had a frown on his face. "Kendall, damn. I love you, girl."

"I love you, too."

I was completely overwhelmed, and I was sure he was, too. The expression on his face said that he was one step away from crying. As I rolled my hips into him, he pinned me against the wall and lifted my legs in the crooks of his arms. He started fucking my shit like it would be the last time. "Price! Fuck!"

I'd cum again and I didn't know how that shit kept happening. I supposed it was the revelations of the night that had taken us to another level. To know that Price loved me had my entire body open. I wanted his love more than anything. I could tell that my admission had done the same to him. As I held onto him, he bounced me on his dick like I weighed nothing. However, watching him watch our fucking turned me on. He was staring at his dick going in and out of me as spit dropped from his mouth. He wanted to make sure I stayed as wet as possible, but he didn't have that shit to worry about.

He had me so open, my shit was on constant pour. The grunts that left him were sexy as hell and I couldn't contain myself either. I'd been screaming almost the entire time. "Kendall, can I nut inside of you?"

I knew that question would be coming. It was too good to pull out. I was on the pill anyway. When he'd asked the question, he'd never looked at me. He'd continued to watch the action. "Yeah, baby."

His head snapped up and he stared in my eyes. "Really?"

"Yeah. I'm on the pill."

"Fuck! I'm close."

"Then let's get it."

I began trying to fuck him back as he lowered his arms. When he did, it gave me more leverage. Fucking each other against that wall was so gratifying, electrifying, and beyond satisfying, I couldn't stop. I wanted more... and more... and more. I would never have enough. "Kendall... fuck!"

With that, we came together and after a moment, my body slid down the wall. Price held onto me to keep me from collapsing to the shower floor. I was spent but not spent enough to deny him if he wanted more. Shit, I wanted more. So, after our shower, that was exactly what I was gonna get... more.

CHAPTER 18

P rice

I was fucking tired, but excited as hell at the same time. Kendall was insatiable last night and hell, I was, too. I loved her and that was hard for me to believe. I'd never fallen that fast before. She was everything I wanted and more. While I knew she could be a little stubborn, because of her persistence that I stayed with her, I knew it was because she'd been on her own for so long. Kendall didn't have to depend on anybody for anything and it had been that way for years. So, she didn't know how to let someone take care of her.

After last night, though, I knew she would be willing to do whatever I wanted her to. She'd said in the heat of passion that I could have whatever I wanted from her. People said things they didn't really mean in the heat of passion. I knew that. But I was gon' remind her of that when I needed to. We'd fucked and made love in positions I hadn't been in in years. Kendall had came so many times, she practically passed out after the last one. I was thanking God that Cassie wasn't there with us, because when I made love to her clit with my tongue, she was so loud, I almost came just from the passion.

As we walked into Texas Children's Hospital, I got antsy. I didn't know what I would see when we got to Cassie. Kendall had told me that Shayla had said she was refusing to eat or talk and had been sleeping a lot. For two weeks, I'd been missing my baby something fierce and now I was finally gonna get to see her again. Grabbing Kendall's hand as we got on the elevator, I pulled her closer to me. "You nervous?"

"A little. I don't know what to expect."

She rubbed my hand between hers, then kissed my cheek. "Everything will be fine. Whatever has happened, we will deal with it and get Cassie back to health and back to the progress she was making."

I nodded my head and thanked God for Kendall's support. Her spirit calmed mine. Once we'd gotten off the elevator and had gotten to the waiting area, I realized it was visitation. After grabbing Kendall's hand once again, I damn near drug her to the ICU unit. When we walked down the halls, a few of the nurses smiled at me. They were happy that we were back as well. Cassie was progressing so much when we were here. Once we were at her door, I could see that she was asleep. Shayla was sitting there rubbing her hand. A look of relief flooded her face when she saw us. She stood from her seat. "Thank you."

I nodded at her. However, she should have known that I wanted to be here. I would never deny doing anything that involved Cassie. Blood or not, she was mine. When I got to her bedside, I could see the dark circles under her eyes. That made my heart hurt. I could tell she'd lost weight and that was saying something. Cassie was already straight up and down, but she did have a little meat on her bones. When I touched her, her eyes popped open. She knew my touch. Her eyes brightened when she looked up at me. "Daddy," she whispered.

"Hey, baby girl. I missed you."

"I missed you, too."

I leaned over and kissed her head. The hair that she did have left was a matted mess. Shayla had at least taken the braids that remained out of her hair, but it didn't look like she'd tried to comb it at all. I was almost sure Kendall would change that this weekend. Cassie lifted one arm to hug me, so I allowed her to embrace me and kiss my cheek. When I stood up straight, I wiped the tears from her eyes. She looked over at Kendall and said, "Hi, Ms. Washington."

"Hi, sweetheart."

I moved over so Kendall could hug her and glanced at Shayla in the process. She was crying. While I hated what she'd done, I knew I needed to talk to her. I gestured with my head for her to step out in the hallway with me. She followed me out and she looked nervous. "Look. I can't go through that shit again. I need you to get something in writing stating that I'm Cassie's legal guardian. I would have been in court forever trying to get her back, because you wanted some money. She's not a dog, Shayla. Look at how what you did affected her."

"I know and I'm sorry. I've already gotten the letter written and notarized. I just ask if I can see her from time to time."

"I don't see why that would be a problem."

She fell against me and hugged me tightly as Kendall glanced at us through the window. There was a slight frown on her face. I smirked because I had yet to see her possessive side. However, I knew she would let this one slide due to the circumstances. Pulling away from Shayla, I looked her in the eyes. "Who's her biological dad? And does he know?"

"He doesn't know. It's King. He's her biological father."

King was the nigga she was messing around with when I first met her. I could feel my anger rising, so I knew I needed to kill the conversation, but she kept going. "I didn't know he was her father until the test said you weren't. I mean... I didn't know for sure which one of you was her father until then. But because I knew it was a possibility, I should have been upfront about it."

I only nodded my head. "Does Cassie know? Does she know I'm not her biological dad?"

"Yes. I had to tell her when she was questioning why you weren't here. I told her that I made you leave. That was part of why she stopped talking to me and stopped eating."

I nodded again, then went back inside Cassie's room. A nurse came in right after me with her breakfast and Cassie smiled. "Are you gonna at least try to eat today, sweetheart?"

Cassie nodded her head with a smile as the nurse set her tray on the table in front of her. My baby ate that breakfast so fast, I thought she was gonna choke. As she ate, the nurse called us into the hallway. "If she does well eating today, we will move her to a regular room tomorrow. Other than her not eating and talking, her bones are healing, and the laceration is almost completely healed. Once she's moved and her legs have healed, we will start rehab. I'm so glad she's eating, though. You must have an amazing effect on her. Glad you're back."

"I'm glad I'm back, too. I'll make sure she eats. We need to get this ball rolling in a positive direction."

"Yes, sir."

She shook my hand, then Shayla's, and we went back in the room. Shayla grabbed her purse and got the letter out and handed it to me, then went to Cassie's bedside. I glanced over the letter to make sure it said what she'd told me earlier. Shayla couldn't be trusted, and she'd proven that to me since she abandoned Cassie. Looking up, I saw her kiss Cassie's forehead and Cassie seemed unfazed. But that was Shayla's fault. She whispered something in her ear and Cassie nodded and smiled at her. After that, Shayla smiled at Kendall, then went around Cassie's bed to hug her. "Thank you."

I'd read her lips, but I couldn't make out what else she said. Whatever it was had caused Kendall to cry. Cassie was still smiling, so whatever Shayla had told Kendall, she'd told Cassie first. Kendall hugged Shayla again and Shayla gave her a letter, too. I could imagine what she'd said now. Shayla waved at Cassie, then turned toward the door and wiped the tears from her eyes. After I'd walked to Cassie's bedside, we watched Shayla leave without a look back. "Baby, why you crying?"

Cassie's eyes brightened. I was sure it was because I'd called Kendall baby. "Shayla told me that she would be happy for Cassie to call me mama, because I'd been more of a mother to her lately than she had and that she trusted me to take care of her."

Cassie was smiling brightly. "How does that make you feel?" I asked.

"Amazing. I've always wanted to be a mother and now, Shayla is giving me the gift of being one."

"What about you, Cassie?"

"Is Ms. Washington your girlfriend?"

"Yeah," I answered, then turned and kissed Kendall on the lips.

"I'm happy to have a mama and daddy that love each other. After the first time Ms. Washington did my hair, I loved her. Aren't you glad you shot your shot, Daddy?"

Kendall and I laughed as Cassie smiled. We were going to be a family and I couldn't be happier in this moment. When we could make that official would be one of the happiest days of my life. So, our first task was getting Cassie's healing progress back on track so we could get her out of this hospital.

"TRICIA AND I ARE GETTING A DIVORCE."

"What? Everything worked out for the best, bruh."

"No. If she's capable of that type of betrayal, what else has she put her nose in? No. Fuck that. I can't trust her. After all these years and I find out that she's a money hungry, backstabbing bitch. That shit was hurtful and embarrassing. It came out in front of Kendall's family that my wife, the only white person in the room, had betrayed her black brother-in-law. You know how that shit looks? People were already quick to judge our marriage, simply because she's white and I'm black. I love black women, but I just happened to fall in love with a white woman." He huffed loudly. "My kids are staying with me, too."

"I hate that, bruh, but I understand."

Karter and his kids had gotten here an hour ago and he had pulled me out in the hallway to talk. It was Saturday afternoon and they were preparing to move Cassie to a regular room. God was so good. She'd been here a little over a month and had progressed tremendously. The only things she seemed to be dealing with now were the broken bones and the liver laceration. The doctor had said that should be a wrap in another week or so. Once she started therapy and had a couple of rounds, then they would let her go home, providing no other issues arose.

When Karter and the kids had come without Tricia, I thought it was because she was embarrassed by her behavior and had refused to come, not knowing how I would react. Karter and Tricia had been married for a long while, so I was still somewhat in shock that he'd ended things with her. Well... I probably shouldn't have been surprised. Karter has always looked out for me and had always had my back, no matter who it was against. Since our parents died, that bond had only gotten stronger.

Kendall and I had been in a solemn mood, because we knew we would be back to a "weekends only" arrangement. With Cassie moving to a regular room, I wouldn't be able to leave the hospital at all now. An adult had to be with her at all times. As Karter and I walked back inside, everyone was giving her kisses. Visitation was just about over, but they were about to move her as well. After kissing her and letting her know that we would see her in a little bit, we headed to the waiting area. The nurses said someone would come get us right before they moved her.

Kendall and I walked hand in hand behind everyone else. The silence between us was choking the hell outta me. I looked over at her. "Baby? You okay?"

"Yeah. I'm trying to be. I wish I didn't have to leave y'all tomorrow, but I'm trying to focus on the time we have now. I don't wanna spend the time we have left today thinking about the time we won't have."

"Right. Before long, we'll be home and you'll be trying to get away from us to get you some free time."

She chuckled. "We'd have to be living together for that to happen."

I rubbed the top of my head. "Living together will only work if you allow me to be the man. It's bad enough it's your house. But if I live there, I gotta take care of majority if not all of the bills. I'm not a weak ass nigga. I can't have no woman taking care of me. That shit nearly ate me up the past couple of weeks."

She took a deep breath. We'd stopped in the hall, right outside of the waiting area. "I know. I'm just so used to taking care of myself. It's hard letting someone do the hard work for me."

I lifted both hands to her face and palmed her cheeks. "Let me be the man. I know it's old fashioned, but that's how I was brought up. A real man takes care of his woman, not the other way around. I love you, Kendall. Let me show you how much I love you by taking that load off you, baby."

I could feel the heat coming from her in my palms and her eyes were locked on mine. "Okay. I'm willing to try. I'll do my best, because I love you, too. And I want us to get to that point one day."

"Yeah. Cassie can't have her mama and daddy living apart for too long."

Her face really turned red. Kendall wrapped her arms around my waist and laid her head on my chest as I rubbed her back and kissed her forehead. "One day, we'll all live together as a family. And it will probably be sooner rather than later."

She took a deep breath and exhaled against me. I caressed her flawless skin, as she lifted her head and looked in my eyes. The goosebumps appeared on her flesh and that shit made a nigga swell up with pride. To know I had that effect on her, assured me of her love and attraction to me. She felt me at depths no one had ever reached, and I wondered what it was about me that deserved all the love she wanted to give me. God had blessed me to find her, and if it weren't for Shayla leaving Cassie with me, I wouldn't have ever found her.

According to Alana, Kendall liked to go out and have a good time occasionally, which was how she met that nigga, West. I rarely went out, because I always had to work, and when I didn't, I tried to spend that time with Cassie. So, I was convinced that we would have never met. For God to bless me with this woman, I had to be doing something right. I was at an all-time high. My daughter was back in my custody and Kendall was my friend, my lover, and my woman. Things couldn't get any better.

CHAPTER 19

K endall

It had been a long ass day, and I just wanted to go home. Leaving Price and Cassie yesterday was hard as hell. I almost called in, but I knew I'd have to face the inevitable anyway. The kids seemed to be as tired as I was. I didn't get home until almost midnight, so I only got about five hours of sleep. Anything under six hours wasn't good for me. I'd been yawning all day and the kids were following suit. We made fun of one another every time it happened. Talking to Price during lunch and my conference period kept me alert, because I wanted to go to sleep so badly.

I gathered my things along with their assignments, then headed to the back where I had to park. I was later than usual and all the parking spots up front were taken. Calling Price, I could feel my body anticipating the feeling I got when I heard his voice. "Hey, sexy," he answered.

"Hey, baby. How are you and Cassie?"

"We're good. We've been doing a lot of talking and joking around. Catching up on what we missed those two weeks we were apart, which wasn't much."

"Right. We didn't do much of anything the entire time."

I continued listening to Price talk about Cassie as I fished inside my bag for my keys. "You need help?"

My body stilled at the sound of the voice. Price asked, "Who was that?"

I dropped the phone in my bag as I turned around. It was West. *Why did this have to happen to me?* When I looked in his eyes, I didn't like what I saw. It wasn't rage or anger, but it was what looked to be strong desire and wanting. "What are you doing here, West? I have a restraining order against you."

"How they gon' put a restraining order on what we have? This attraction is so strong, nobody can contain it. I can't contain it! Kendall, you can't tell me you don't feel the same way!"

I could vaguely here Price on the phone still and it sounded like he was panicking. I could hear an operator say, *9-1-1, what is your emergency?* He'd called 9-1-1 on three-way. Smart thinking. "West, I don't feel for you the way you feel for me. I can't believe you showed up at my job again. Mae Jones-Clark is gonna fire me and I won't be able to get a job in all of BISD."

I was doing my best to drop my whereabouts. Hopefully, it didn't sound too suspect. "What do you mean you don't feel for me the way I feel for you? This shit is one-sided!"

"West, please calm down," I said, trying to remain calm.

"Don't tell me to calm down!"

He slapped the piss out of me, and I was in shock. There was a ringing in my ear, and I knew that I would have a bruise there. "I thought you felt for me," I asked, trying to play on his emotions.

"I do! Look what'chu made me do! Find your keys and get in the car."

I dug around in my bag and finally found my keys. I could have shot myself for not having my keys out before going outside. He walked around the car and hurriedly pulled the handle as I unlocked it. *Fuck!* He was a little smarter than what I gave him credit for. "Get in the car, Kendall!"

I looked back at the school and was about to make a run for it until he pulled a gun from his waistband. "Get your ass in the car. I'm not gonna tell you again."

I quickly did as he said. "West, why do you have a gun?"

"Because I knew you would need some persuading. You women today are so damn smart-mouthed and defiant. We are supposed to handle things and you are supposed to be submissive!" he scratched his head with his free hand. "Drive to your house."

Just as he said that, I felt something warm between my legs. For a minute I thought I'd pissed on myself. "Shit!"

It wasn't piss. I'd started my damn cycle without warning. It was about that time, but fuck! I usually at least cramped first. "What's wrong?"

"I started my period."

"Well, I'll have to clean you up when we get to your place," he said with a smirk on his face.

My nerves were on edge and I could vaguely hear Price telling me he loved me. "West, I have a boyfriend and we're in love."

"Shut up! I don't wanna hear shit about a boyfriend! Kendall, I need you to stop fucking with me!"

I remained silent the rest of the way home. My hope was that they would catch up to us before we got to my house. Price was the only man that I wanted to see me naked. This muthafucka had stressed me right into my cycle. I'd never been so scared in my life. My head was pounding, and I was trembling like crazy. "I hate I have to do this just for you to see how much I care for you, Kendall. My mama keeps telling me to let you go and take my medicine, but she doesn't know what it feels like to want someone that doesn't seem to realize how much they want you, too. I know you want me. I can feel it."

When we got to my street, I could see the police cars and I

couldn't be more grateful. They'd blocked my driveway and the street past my house. When I looked in the rearview mirror, there were two cars of cops behind me. "Why are they all here? I only want to spend time with you, Kendall!"

He began scratching his head with that gun and I was nervous as hell. Secondly, I was grateful as hell that my Bluetooth didn't pick up. I'd been having problems with it, but I just knew that it would work fine when I didn't need it to. It didn't let me down. "What do you want me to do, West?"

He pointed the gun at me and said, "I want you to kiss me, Kendall, so you can feel what I feel."

My entire body was trembling, and I knew that if I didn't do what he said, he could possibly shoot me. As I leaned toward him, I noticed some shit that made me wanna fuck him up. It was a damn water gun. It didn't have the typical orange or red tip, nor trigger, but I could see the water leaking from it. That ignorant ass muthafucka. "West. I want to do what you asked of me, but I don't want to feel like I'm cheating on my boyfriend. So, shoot me."

I could hear Price practically screaming on the phone. West heard it, too. "Get that phone!"

I refused. "No! Shoot me!"

He was starting to get nervous. I swear that fucking gun looked so real. The gun was trembling along with his hand. "Don't make me do this, Kendall!"

"Do it! Don't be weak!"

I literally wanted to laugh at his ass at this point. Fear was no longer running through my body. I had a combination of humor, anger, and sadness running through me. He could die for this shit. "West, I know that's a water gun."

I said that mostly so no one would shoot him. The operator was probably still on the phone and could relay that message to the officers. They were approaching my car as I sat there with a mentally disturbed West. He would be doing some time. Without a doubt, this time. I was already feeling emotional today, but then this and my period had violently kicked me off the cliff. How in the fuck did I attract this looney? He showed no signs of this in the club. Maybe he was medicated then.

I was about to get out of my car, but he yanked my arm, pulling me back. Felt like he pulled that shit out of the socket, it hurt so bad. Grabbing a handful of my hair, he said, "You don't follow instructions very well. Get that phone! This is not a water gun. I will use it to prove that to you!"

I rolled my eyes, then got my bag out the backseat. When I got the phone out, he snatched it out of my hand. "Is this Price?"

"This is a 9-1-1 operator..."

Before she could continue, he ended the call, then punched me in the nose. This time, I punched his ass back. My fist landed in his eye. "You are not going to keep hitting me with no consequence!"

I went wild on his ass, causing him to drop the gun to the floor. The police rushed the car and drug him out with a stunned look on his face. I was sure he wasn't expecting me to fight him back. Now that the police had him, I was curious about that damn gun. Before I could reach for it, a police officer was there to help me out of the car. I accepted his help and he led me to the porch of my house where there was a place to sit.

They'd gotten West handcuffed and in the back of a cop car. My face was hurting, and I wanted to look at the damage, but I'd wait until I was alone. Alone. *Would I be okay with being alone?* I was going to have to call Alana and P. The officer sat next to me and another stood on the porch across from us. There was record of the first attempt and restraining order. After I told them the details of what happened this time, I had to know. "Was that a real gun or was it a water gun?"

The officers looked at one another, then back at me. "It was a real gun. We aren't sure why it was wet, but it was real."

"Oh God. He could've killed me."

My body started to tremble, and I brought my hands to my face, but instantly regretted that. My face hurt so bad and there was a little blood on my hands. "Ma'am, I think you should go to the hospital. Your nose is starting to swell. Is there anyone you want us to call?"

I nodded my head and gave them Alana's number. However, calling Price was the only thing on my mind. I knew he was worried sick. As I walked to the ambulance, I made a pit stop to my car for my bag, keys and phone. When I bent over, it felt like my brain had somehow eased down to my nose. The shit was painful. Once I got everything, I got in the ambulance and they looked at my nose. "Let me make a call first. I probably won't want to talk once you touch it."

They stood back and allowed me to make my call. Before the phone even rang on my end, Price answered, sounding hysterical. "Hello? Kendall?"

"Hey, baby. I'm okay, but I think my nose might be broken."

"Shit. I wish I could be there. I was so damned scared. When you said he had a gun, I almost lost it. Was it real or a water gun like you thought?"

"I thought it was a water gun, so when he hit me again, I fought his ass. I later found out that the gun was indeed real."

"Shit. He could've killed you. Baby... fuck. I need you close to me. You and Cassie mean the world to me and when I can't protect y'all, I feel helpless. Please ask Alana if she can bring you to Houston. I need to be able to take care of you. Please..."

I could hear how emotional he was becoming. I was emotional as well. "Okay. I'll ask her. I'm gonna have to take off anyway. I hate that you have all this stress on you, Price."

"I'll feel better once you're here. I have to go, baby, because Cassie is starting to wake up. I don't want her to know that something's wrong just yet."

"Okay. I'll try to call you after they do whatever they're about to do to my nose, but I can't make any promises. If I can't call, I'll have Alana call."

"Okay, baby. I love you." He exhaled. "Thank God you're okay."

"I love you, too. See you soon."

I ended the call and the paramedic approached me and had me

put my head back. He informed me that he would have to reset it. The tears sprang from my eyes, although he hadn't done a thing yet. But dear Lord baby Jesus when he did, I wanted to scream. As I sat there taking deep breaths, I saw Alana running toward me, then P right behind her. When they got to me, they both grabbed one of my hands as I sat there with my eyes closed. "Doll, my God. I'm so sorry. I would have never thought he would be capable of this."

Peyton kissed me on the cheek as Alana kissed my hand. "What do you need from us, Ken? Do you want us to stay with you tonight?"

"Can y'all take me to Houston? Price wants me with him as soon as possible. I wanna be with him, too."

"Are y'all in love, sis?"

"Yeah."

"I knew it was coming. I love how y'all are together. It's like you can't focus on anything else. You're so happy. I'm happy that you've found love. I will gladly take you to him. Price is a good man. So, when is the wedding?"

That was just like Alana to try to take my mind off what had happened. I was grateful for that right now. Keeping my mind on Price and Cassie, kept me from panicking. While they giggled, I smiled slightly. Even that hurt my face. "Sorry, Kendall. I'll follow y'all to the hospital."

Peyton rode in the ambulance with me to the hospital and she held my hand the entire time. Before we could get there though, she said, "I saw Karter at the grocery store."

I frowned slightly. I didn't know what the importance of her telling me was, so I said, "Oh okay."

"He asked me for my number. He said he and his wife broke up."

Although I was shocked, I couldn't portray that with as badly as my face was throbbing. "Really? What about Lawrence?"

Lawrence was her boyfriend. They'd been together for at least six months. While we hadn't been talking much since I'd been with Price, I was sure she would have told me that they broke up. "We broke up two weeks ago. I didn't want to bother you, because y'all had enough going on. It was the same weekend we all came over because Cassie's mother had acted an ass."

"Wow, P. I'm sorry. But no matter how much I have going on, you can always talk to me. There's always room for you and Alana. I love y'all."

"I love you, too, Doll."

"So, what are you gonna do?"

"I gave him my number. He hasn't called yet, though. That was a couple of days ago."

"His breakup is still pretty fresh. Maybe he's still dealing with that."

"Yeah."

Once we'd gotten to the hospital, they ran x-rays of my face and shoulder. My shoulder was still somewhat sore from when he'd yanked me in the car to keep me from getting out. As we waited for the doctor to tell me the results, Alana updated me on the guy she'd been talking to. They were talking about taking things to the next level and I was happy for her as well. She promised to bring him around more. She said that he wanted to come around, but she would always tell him no. I could only shake my head at her stubbornness. She was just like our mama. I was too, until I met Price. From the day I first laid eyes on him, he'd taken me on a slow, sensual filled ride to ecstasy.

It turned out that everything was okay, and the only issue was my nose. Since the paramedic had reset it, it only needed to heal, and they prescribed me some pain meds. Once we filled the prescriptions, went to my house so I could shower and pack a bag, we headed to Houston. As Alana drove, I looked in my compact mirror to see that my eyes were starting to blacken a little bit. The doctor had told me that could happen, but that it should go away within a week or two. It would take two to three weeks for my nose to heal completely. It was so hard to breathe out of my nostrils, but I knew that the worst of it was over. Due to the effects of the pain medication, I drifted off to sleep while thoughts of Price filled my mind.

CHAPTER 20

P rice

I'D BEEN PACING for almost an hour. When Alana called me and said they were on their way and that Kendall was doped up, talking crazy, I couldn't help but feel more at ease. However, it had been two more hours since that call, and they should have been here by now. *Maybe they weren't really on their way.* Kendall had to pack clothes and toiletries. I didn't know how long she would be staying, but I knew she would at least be here for the rest of the week. Tomorrow, I'd let her take my truck, so she could get a hotel room. This little sofa bed I was sleeping on, wouldn't offer her any comfort, but I needed her near me.

Just as I was about to call Alana to see where they were, my phone started to ring. Cassie stirred as she did earlier, making me think she was gonna wake up, only for her to try to change positions. This time her eyes slowly opened, and she smiled at me as I answered the phone. "Hello?"

"Hey, Price. It's Alana. Sorry, it took us a little longer. It took Kendall forever to pack clothes. She was so doped up. We're parking and should be up there in a little bit."

"Okay. Yeah, I was just about to call you. I've been pacing for the past fifteen minutes."

"Aww. How sweet."

I slightly rolled my eyes. Alana was a mess. "Man, whatever. Just get my baby up here."

"Aight, aight."

She giggled as she ended the call. I became slightly worried, because I didn't know exactly what I would see when she got up here. She told me that her nose was possibly broken, and Alana told me they had to reset it, but I didn't ask if there were other bruises. "Daddy, who's coming?"

"Kendall... I mean Ms. Washington."

"You mean Mama?"

I smiled at my baby girl and lowered my head. I still wasn't used to her calling Kendall mama. "Yeah. Umm... she got hurt. A man tried to hurt her really bad, but she's still able to walk and talk. Her face is just bruised up, because he broke her nose."

"Oh no..." she said softly as the tears started to fall from her eyes.

"Don't worry, baby. She's gonna be okay. I just didn't want you to be surprised when you saw her."

I walked over to her bedside and rubbed her hair, then kissed her head. Wiping away her tears, I again kissed her forehead as there was a knock at the door. Shortly after, the nurse came in to check Cassie's vitals and asked her how she was feeling. She also informed me that they would get her out of bed to sit in a wheelchair. Cassie seemed to get excited about that. I knew she had to be tired of that bed. Before the nurse could leave, Alana peeked her head in. "What'chu peeking for? Get my baby in here."

She rolled her eyes and walked in with Kendall right behind her. I almost lost my shit when I saw her face. That muthafucka better stay locked up or I was gon' have something for his ass. Pulling her in

CHAPTER 20 | 151

my arms, I swallowed the lump in my throat. "Baby, I'm so sorry this happened to you. West gon' have some shit to deal with when I get ahold of him."

"No. It's over. We need you, so you can't be going all Rambo and shit," Kendall whispered.

I could tell she was still a little high. Just the way she said 'going all Rambo' let me know that. I didn't say anything about a gun, but baby girl went to the extreme like I was going to blow some shit up. I chuckled a bit, then brought her to Cassie's bed. Her state of mind had calmed me down some. When she got to the bed, Cassie looked at her sadly. "Mama, are you okay?"

By Kendall's facial expression, I could tell she hadn't got used to Cassie calling her mama either. She smiled slightly. "I'm okay, sweetheart. It looks bad though, huh?"

"Yes ma'am. Are you gonna stay with us?"

"Yes. I'm staying tonight, then I will probably get a hotel room. But I'll be here every day for the next two weeks."

Cassie smiled even bigger than she was. I hadn't shown Cassie pictures of how she looked when she first got here, but she had a broken nose as well. Hers had healed while she was in a medically induced coma. Alana and Peyton had sat on the couch, so I sat in the recliner and beckoned Kendall to come sit on my lap. When she did, I kissed her lips softly. Her face was somewhat swollen around her nose and eyes and I could see the light bruising on her cheek. Not to mention, the flesh around her eyes was darkened.

I gently stroked her cheek with my fingertips. "Did the police let you know when he would be arraigned?"

"In the morning."

I could tell she was tired. Alana and Peyton stood from the couch and pulled the bed out, then got the linen from the closet for her. Once they'd made her bed for the night, I helped her to her feet and brought her to it. After she sat, I took off her shoes. She wiggled her toes and smiled at me. I was glad they'd gotten her showered while they were in Beaumont. With as tired as she was, it would have been difficult to do that here. I whispered in her ear, "I love you, baby."

"I love you, too."

"Do you want me to take your bra off?"

"No. I'm on my period, though. So, I should probably go check myself before I go to sleep."

"I'll take her, Price," Peyton said.

I was grateful she said that, because I didn't know what to do about that situation. I was dreading the day that Cassie would start hers. Seeing my baby becoming a woman wasn't something I was looking forward to. That thought made me even more grateful to have Kendall in our lives. Once she came out of the bathroom, she smiled at me. "I'm good. No leakage."

I lowered my head and chuckled silently while Cassie frowned slightly. Her mind was probably trying to figure out just what Kendall was talking about. If she didn't ask any questions, then I wouldn't be volunteering any information either. That conversation would be left to one of the women in our lives now. As she got situated on the couch, Alana giggled quietly. I shook my head slowly. She could find humor in damn near anything. As I watched my love get situated, my phone started to ring. Pulling it from my pocket, I saw it was my brother. "Hello?"

"What's up, bruh? How are y'all?"

"We're good. How are y'all?"

"It's a struggle but we're okay. Tricia has been calling nonstop. The kids are both upset about what she did, especially Bri. She misses her mom, but at the same time, she feels like I do; like she can't trust her."

"I can understand that. Well, Kendall's back here with me. That..." I glanced over at Cassie to see her watching Kendall. "That nigga assaulted her," I said in a lower voice.

"Man, what the fuck is up with him?"

"I don't know, but that muthafucka better be glad he in jail."

"What's his name? I'm gon' keep his ass on my radar."

"West... West McFall, I think."

"What the fuck? You serious?"

"Yeah. You know him?"

"Hell, yeah. That nigga was tryna holla at Tricia a couple of years back. That was the dude we had to press charges against."

"What the fuck? I never knew his name. How ironic is it that he would try both of our women?"

"I know, right? You think it's something we need to look into?"

"Well, I don't know. He met Kendall before I did at a jazz club. Where did he meet Tricia?"

"I think he saw her at the grocery store or something like that. Maybe it's just a coincidence."

My mind was running a damn marathon. I was always thinking ahead, but now even more so since Shayla and Tricia had pulled their lil stunts. My baby's welfare and safety was in jeopardy, so I couldn't afford to slip up. It could be nothing, but my eyes would be open to spot bullshit easily. "I already know you thinking. Concentrate on those women. I'll be scoping shit out."

"You damn right I'm thinking," I said as I noticed Alana and Peyton standing to their feet.

"How did Kendall get there? She drove herself?"

"Naw. Alana and Peyton brought her."

"Word? Tell P I said what's up."

I frowned slightly. "Man... you move fast, huh?"

When I said that, Peyton glanced over at me. Her skin turned slightly red as she not so secretly watched me. "Karter told me to tell you hello, P."

She blushed as Alana looked from her to me with a smirk on her face. Clearly, I was the last one to know about these developments. "Karter, how dare you keep me in the dark?"

"Ain't nothing happened. I saw her in the grocery store a couple of days ago and asked her for her number. I ain't even called her yet. What did she say?"

"Nothing. She just smiled."

"Well, that's a good sign. Tell her that I will call her in a little while."

"Naw. 'Cause then Alana will be all in y'all's business."

Alana laughed loudly, then covered her mouth. "Shut up, Price!" she said in a hushed tone. "I am not that nosy. I'll wait 'til they get off the phone and let P fill me in."

It was my turn to laugh as Peyton turned even redder. She finally said, "Tell him to call me in thirty minutes."

"You heard her?"

"Yep. I can't wait to talk to her. She's a sweet woman."

"Yep. So, don't mess up. Kendall and Alana ain't 'bout to have me all hemmed up for something you did."

He laughed. I had been talking to Karter almost every day and this was my first time hearing him laugh in a while. If Peyton had him feeling like that already, then who was I to stand in the way of that? It didn't mean they had to embark on a relationship but wasn't nothing wrong with them getting to know one another and developing a friendship. Suddenly, Kendall snored loudly. Cassie laughed so hard. We'd all turned toward her with frowns on our faces. "See what y'all got to look forward to tonight," Alana said.

"It gotta be that pain medicine, because we stayed together for two weeks and I ain't never heard nothing like that come out of her. That sounded like a damn lawn mower."

Everybody laughed as I continued to frown. Hell, I was gon' need a pain shot before it was all over with. Finally, I joined them as I watched Kendall lay there with her mouth wide opened. Alana took her phone from her pocket and took a picture of her. I was pretty sure it would be for blackmail purposes in the future. My attention then went back to Cassie as she frowned and held her chest. I rushed to her. "Baby, you okay?"

"My chest hurts."

"You still have broken ribs baby. While they're healing, they aren't healed all the way. So that hard laugh probably caused that."

I called the nurse as Peyton and Alana stood there making sure

Cassie was okay. "We're gonna go, Price. We both have work in the morning."

"Okay. Thanks for bringing my baby, although I don't know who in the hell she is right now."

They both laughed as Peyton gave me Kendall's pain meds. I put them in my pocket and hugged the two of them as the nurse came in to give Cassie some pain meds through her IV. Within minutes, she was out.

"Mr. Daniels?"

"Yes."

"This is District Attorney Jamie Holcomb. How's Cassie doing?"

"She's doing well. She's been progressing so quickly, that the doctors here are baffled. But our God is a healer and he's performing a miraculous work in Cassie."

"That's amazing. When I saw that baby, I was scared. I must admit, I didn't think she would make it."

"I was beyond scared, but I had to keep the faith and be strong for her."

"I wanted to let you know that the young man that hit her would be going to court tomorrow morning. He also wrote a letter to you and one to Cassie. I didn't know if you wanted to accept it or not."

My mind wanted to say, *fuck him.* But my heart was saying something totally different. I was no longer angry at him for what he'd done to my baby. While no explanation he gave me would make me feel any better about the situation, I'd forgiven him. God had spared Cassie and through this, He brought me closer to Him. "I'll accept them."

"Okay. I also wanted you to be aware of the charges. He's being charged with vehicular assault and operating a vehicle at unsafe speeds. You can also file civil charges to pay for her medical bills and pain and suffering."

I knew that would be a waste of time. While I would probably win, where would the money come from? While I knew they would garnish his wages if they had to, it would take me forever to get the money from that. "Naw. I don't even want to deal with the process."

"Okay. Well, what about the apartment complex? Your neighbor told me that a few of you had been complaining to the complex to do something about the speeding cars. You could file a civil suit against them."

Now, there was a thought. People sped through the complex all the time. Without speed bumps, it was impossible to get them to slow down. "That's something I'd be interested in doing. Had they put in speed bumps to ensure the safety of their residents, my baby wouldn't be here all broken up."

"I agree. I'll get to work on that for you."

"I don't need a private attorney for that?"

"Nope. I'm gonna handle it for you. Don't ask me why, because I don't even know. All I know is that I feel moved to do so. I'll be in touch."

"Thank you. I really appreciate it."

"If you can, I would move out of the complex. Just to be sure they don't try to retaliate against you by putting you out."

"Okay. I'll get my brother to move my things into storage. Thanks again."

When I ended the call, Kendall was sitting on the little couch looking at me. I could tell she was in pain, now. Last night she'd been hopped up on pain meds. "Good morning, baby. How you feeling?"

"Horrible," she said softly.

I grabbed the pill bottle from Cassie's table and gave them to her. After kissing her forehead, I said, "Peyton left those for you."

"Thanks."

She got up from the couch and a soft groan left her lips. I went to her luggage and fished out her toothpaste and toothbrush, so she didn't have to bend over and handed them to her. "Thank you, Price."

I hugged her loosely and she laid her head on my chest for a moment. She seemed to be feeling sensitive and somewhat emotional. I knew she would be though, once those meds wore off. When she lifted her head, I swiped the tears from her cheeks. "Everything's gon' be okay, baby. I got'chu."

"I love you, Price."

"I love you, too."

"You were speaking to a detective?"

"Yeah."

I ran down the conversation with the detective to Kendall as she brushed her teeth. When she was done, she said, "That's good news. What do you think the letters will say other than he's sorry?"

"I don't know, that's why I accepted them. I'm curious."

She nodded slightly, then wet a towel to wash her face. Watching her glide the towel along her face gently, was only making me angry, but the way she looked at herself in the mirror when she first walked in was heartbreaking. I didn't know if she hadn't seen herself in the mirror or if she didn't remember because of the pain meds, but whatever the case, it was killing her. Her chest began to heave like she was trying to hold in her cries. Pulling her to me again, I said, "Baby, it's gonna heal. Okay? You gon' get through this. I hate what he did to you and if I could, I'd spring his ass outta that jail and fuck him up."

Before she could respond, there was a knock at the door. Noticing it was almost eight, I knew it was probably me and Cassie's breakfast trays. Leaving Kendall in the restroom, I went into the room to open the door. Sure enough, it was dietary bringing our trays, just as I figured. Cassie was rubbing her eyes as I sat her breakfast in front of her. To say it was hospital food, it was pretty decent. They'd given her pancakes, eggs, two strips of bacon, and fruit. Her appetite had been great, so I was grateful for that.

Kendall came out of the bathroom and Cassie said, "Good morning, Mommy."

Man... I didn't know why every time she called Kendall mommy it affected me like it was the first time. My heart was soft as shit and

Kendall looked like she wanted to cry all over again. "Good morning, sweetheart. How are you feeling?"

"I feel okay. How is your nose feeling?"

"It hurts, but I can handle it. You know why?"

"Why?"

"Because I have you for a daughter."

"Aight, aight. Y'all cut it out," I said as I wiped my face like I'd been crying.

They both giggled. "Aww, daddy we're sorry," Kendall said.

She hugged me around my waist. "Daddy, huh? You better cut that shit out before I call for Cassie a pain shot and fuck the shit out of you in that bathroom."

Her face turned red and her body trembled, but she had no words. I chuckled as I went to the breakfast tray they brought for me, to see what was on it. "Daddy, you'll cut my pancake?"

"Of course." I began cutting her pancake, then turned my attention to Kendall. "Baby, you want what's on my tray or you want something else? I'll go down to the cafeteria and get us something else if you don't want that."

They'd done biscuits and gravy and I couldn't stand that shit. Kendall lifted the lid and turned her lip up. "I don't like biscuits and gravy."

"Good. That's one food I know you will never cook, and I won't have to pretend to like."

She stared at me seriously until I started laughing. Cassie smiled while chewing her food, watching me dodge Kendall's slaps. "I was just kidding, baby."

I eventually stopped dodging her and let her slap my arm twice. She lifted her arms in the air like she was the champ, causing Cassie to giggle. I could see Cassie being extra careful not to laugh too hard. Small steps. Just the fact that she could laugh at all was a blessing in itself. "Aight, you win. What'chu wanna eat?"

"I like biscuits, just not with gravy, pancakes, breakfast burritos, and lots of other things. So, I should be okay with whatever you get. If you want to be sure, just call me."

"Okay. Cassie, you want anything while I'm going down?"

"Can you buy me some Doritos?"

"Yep. You want a Fanta Strawberry if they have it?"

She smiled. "Yes, sir, or a Sprite."

"Aight. Let me take care of my queen and princess. I'll be right back."

When I walked out the door, my face became serious. It was hard pretending to be happy when all I could think about was killing that nigga that fucked Kendall's nose up. Every time I looked at her, I was ready to draw blood. Hopefully with time, that feeling would dissipate, like it had with Cassie.

CHAPTER 21

K endall

It had been two weeks and I was getting ready for work. The detective had assured me that West was still in jail. The judge had set his trial for a month from now. He was being charged with assault, kidnapping, and threatening deadly force. The detective told me he could get as much as ten years in prison unless a deal was put on the table. My nose had healed but the inward scars were still fresh as I drove to work. Price had called the police department to send a car to escort me to school. I was grateful for that.

Cassie was doing extremely well. They'd gotten her out of the bed to see how comfortable she would be sitting in a chair. Her liver was completely healed and so were her ribs. She was still tender there, but the doctor had said that the x-rays looked amazing. I'd done my best to brush her hair. I didn't want to put any product in it, since I couldn't wash it. Her hair was filthy. I did my best to clean it with a dry wash, then just greased her scalp. I would have to cut her hair, though.

While her mother was there, she'd cut the braids out of her hair and cut some of her hair as well. I didn't understand how she'd taken care of her for eight years on her own. Not only that, but maybe a fourth of her head was shaved in the back due to a laceration. The doctor said if Cassie continued to progress the way she was, they may be sending her home next week. I was beyond happy, because they would be living with me. Price had gotten his brother to pack up his apartment, and Alana had come got me last weekend so I could get my car and open my house for Karter to bring Cassie and Price's clothes.

My house was a three-bedroom, so Cassie would be happy to know that I had a place for all her toys and dollhouse. I'd gotten everything organized. Price's gaming system was on the big screen, so I knew he would love that. My mind was also prepared to let him pay bills. He said that was the only way this would work. At first, he was talking about getting another apartment. I literally begged him to move in with me. Once I convinced him that it would be easier for Cassie to live in my house than a cramped apartment, he was sold.

I'd had Peyton stay in the house with me when I got back two nights ago. She didn't work on weekends, so she didn't mind. Alana had stayed one night with us as well. The night Alana stayed over, Peyton had stayed on the phone with Karter almost the entire night. We grilled the hell out of her ass, too. She said they were just getting to know each other, and he'd asked to take her out Friday night. She'd agreed and couldn't wait to spend more time getting to know him. From the way it seemed, they got along well. However, Peyton was so easy to get along with. Sometimes, she was so sweet, she made me sick.

When I got to the school, I called Price. He told me when I got there and was walking from my car to the door to call him. Had he not been on the phone with me that day, that whole situation could have gone so differently. My phone would have been in my bag, so I wouldn't have had access to it. I was just surprised that West hadn't heard the noise on my phone at first to know that it hadn't disconnected. "Hello?"

"Hey, baby. I'm leaving the parking lot."

"How do you feel?"

"I feel okay, since you're on the phone. Once I'm inside, I'm sure I'll be okay, too."

"Well, Karter is going to come to escort you to your car when you get off. Normally he picked Cassie up from school, so I know he'll be able to get to you in time."

"Yeah. I won't have duty for a while because of the incident."

"Good. They need to have security patrolling that lot anyway, since part of it is behind the building."

"Yeah. My principal already sent in the request. She said my assault was on the news. So, that alone forces them to do something about it, especially since the news highlighted that the area where I was parked wasn't visible from the road."

"Well, that's good. Someone wants to talk to you."

"Okay."

"Hey, Mama. Have a good day at school."

"I will. Is it okay if we call you later, so everyone can hear your voice? When I came back to school the last time, they were really concerned about you and wanted to know if they could talk to you when you were feeling better."

"What time? So, I can tell Daddy to make sure I'm awake."

I smiled. She was so grownup for her age. Her height already made her look older than what she was, but her intellect made her seem older even when you knew her age. "We'll call in about the next hour, once everyone is here and situated."

"Okay. Mama?"

"Yes, sweetheart?"

"I love you."

I closed my eyes briefly. It was still unbelievable how God had given me this precious angel to see after and be responsible for. Not only did he give her to me, but he had her comfortable enough with me to call me mama. And when she said mommy, it literally melted my insides. For some reason, mommy was even more endearing. "I love you, too, baby."

"Kendall?"

"I'm still here, but I have to go. The kids will be arriving soon; within the next ten minutes."

"Okay, baby. Have a good day. I love you."

"I love you too, Price."

When I ended the call, I still sat there for five minutes, thanking God for His mercy. The last time I was here could have been the very last time, but He didn't see fit to let my life end that way. I was blessed beyond measure, with life and a beautiful family to love and enjoy spending time with.

As the kids arrived, they hugged me tightly and were all glad I was back. While they got their things put away, I looked over some of the notes the sub left me. I'd written their DOL on the dry erase board, so they were working on that. The substitute didn't seem to have any problems, so that was a good thing. She'd gotten lesson plans from one of the other third grade teachers and carried on with my class. I was extremely grateful for that.

Once they'd all placed their papers in the basket and had been seated, I said, "I have a surprise for you guys. All of you gather around my desk."

They didn't hesitate. They all sprang from their chairs as I pulled out my cell phone and called Price. I expected him to answer, but instead, Cassie answered, "Hello?"

I mouthed to the class to say hello to Cassie and directed them to all say it at the same time. "Hi, Cassie!" they all said in unison.

She giggled. "Hi, everybody."

"Cassie are you at home?"

"No. I'm still in the hospital."

"Wow. You've been in the hospital a long time. This is Laney! I miss you!"

Laney was the little girl she played with during recess all the time. "Hi, Laney! I miss you, too!"

"Is it true you got hit by a truck?" one of the boys asked.

"Yes."

"You're strong, Cassie!" another boy said.

They all laughed, and Cassie did, too. "That's what my daddy says all the time."

I could hear her yawning. I told the kids to tell her bye, so she could get some rest, and that we would call her another time. None of them were ready to say goodbye, but they did so and took their seats. One of the girls raised her hand. "Yes, ma'am?"

"Did the man that hit Cassie get in trouble?"

"Yes, he did. He's gone to jail and will stay there for seven years."

"Did he say he was sorry?"

"Yes."

My mind went back to the day Price had received the letters. Cassie's letter had a picture of a beautifully drawn unicorn. Her letter simply said that he was sorry, and he hoped that she could forgive him for hurting her. She'd looked at her dad and said, *It's okay. I forgive him.*

That had caused the tears to fall from my eyes. But when I read Price's letter, I couldn't hold it together. He'd said that he deserved more than what they were threatening him with for almost killing one of God's precious angels. He also went on to say how he'd just gotten into it with his son's mother and how he was ready to choke the hell out of her. To keep from doing that, he'd gotten in his truck and sped off. When he saw Cassie, he slammed on the brake, but it wasn't quick enough to keep from hitting her.

He'd apologized so much in the letter and begged for Price's forgiveness so much, it tore me up on the inside. I could imagine the tears flowing from his eyes as he wrote it. The nightmares that were probably plaguing him every night was probably too much for him to bear. I couldn't imagine how I would feel if I had hit a kid. He said he'd been praying every night that God would spare her and restore the quality of life she once had. While he had been the one to hurt Cassie, I couldn't help but feel sorry for him. He'd made a horrible decision to speed through that apartment complex and he could have cost Cassie her life.

However, I didn't believe he was a bad person. For starters, he didn't have to write the letters to Price and Cassie, but he did. Cassie was coloring the unicorn before Price could finish reading his letter. Secondly, he wasn't looking for a reason to reduce his sentence. He'd pled guilty without a deal being on the table. That spoke of the goodness in his heart.

Before I knew it, it was lunch time and I was starving. Sitting at the hospital, Price and I were always snacking on something. There wasn't much else to do but sit there and watch movies with Cassie or sleep. When I'd gotten home and weighed myself, I'd gained a whole five pounds. After going to the lounge to heat up my potato soup, I came back to my classroom and called Price. "Hey, baby. How's your day going?"

"It's going well. The kids were so excited to hear from Cassie."

"She was excited, too. She'd fall asleep, then wake up talking about school, then fall back to sleep."

He chuckled. "Is she sleeping now?"

"Yeah. They worked baby girl to death, today. Lifting her legs for what seemed like a good thirty minutes. The therapist assured me it had only been fifteen. She was crying, because she was so tired, but I rooted for her to keep going. I explained to her how it was critical to build up her strength, so she could walk again. But on the inside, it was killing me to see my baby in so much pain and crying."

"Oh, I can imagine. I probably would have been crying with her."

"They're going to take her to the pool tomorrow. That heat, along with the resistance will be good for her."

"Yeah, it will be. If I could, I'd come get in the water with her. I'm thinking about enrolling in a water aerobics class. I gained five pounds while I was up there. Can you believe that?"

"Yep. Wait until I start digging you out again. Those hips gon' spread like butter on hot toast."

I slightly rolled my eyes. "If you say so."

"You don't think so? You know I'm gon' be digging that out every night, once I put Cassie to bed."

I moaned softly. "I know you will, Price. I can't wait."

GETTING home that first day after work had proven to be the hardest thing I'd ever done. I was so paranoid, even though Karter was right behind me the entire way. He'd even watched me go in the house and lock the door. But by the time I'd gotten inside, I was practically hyperventilating. It had gotten easier over the past week and a half. But today, I was beyond excited, because Price and Cassie were coming home. I'd cleaned the entire house yesterday evening and started a roast in my slow cooker so it could cook overnight.

This morning I'd cooked rice, green beans, made a potato salad, and baked a cake. I only had to put icing on the cake when I got home. My body was sore as hell from preparing for their arrival. Alana was off today, so she promised to be there when they arrived. My parents said they would be there as well. I couldn't wait until I got off, so I could welcome them home. We'd talked during my conference period and they were almost in Beaumont. Teaching these kids for the last couple of hours was out. They could color for the rest of the evening.

I'd been sure to look extra snazzy today, just for him. I'd worn a black leather skirt, that clung to my curves with a black and crimson, ruffled shirt and a black blazer to hide my curves. The skirt was some-what short and was pushing the limits of the dress code, but today, I didn't even care. As long as Price was drooling over my thick ass legs, that was all that mattered. While the kids colored, I touched up my makeup and made sure every straw curl was in place. Then, I stood from my desk and cleaned the board and prepared for tomorrow's lesson.

By the time all of that was done, it was time to go home. I practically pushed those kids out the room so I could get to my loves. *My family.* My parents were concerned at first, hoping that Price wasn't using me. When I told them that it was my idea and how he'd refused unless I allowed him to pay the bills, they relaxed. My parents knew that I had been independent for a while and did a lot of things for myself even when I was living under their roof. So, I could understand their concern and hesitancy accepting the level Price and I were moving to.

We'd been together for almost two months now and I knew that he was it for me. Price Daniels...

He knew how to caress me without even touching me.

He knew how to speak to me without opening his mouth.

He made love to me without being in the same room.

He drove me to euphoria without an orgasmic release.

I needed him and Cassie in my life. There was no doubt about that. I felt a sense of fulfillment with them that I had never felt and that was a feeling I never wanted to let go of. As I drove home, I realized I'd been smiling the whole time I was driving. I laughed at myself and bit my bottom lip like he liked me to. Whenever I did that in his presence, he would lick his lips and set my soul ablaze.

When I turned in my driveway and saw all the cars along the side of the road, I got even more excited! My parents were here, along with Alana and Karter. Peyton was here as well, and there was probably a nurse or home health provider and therapist. Cassie would have a nurse and therapist come to her every day until she was walking on her own. She had a long road ahead, but half the battle was already fought. I jumped out my car and almost ran to the back door. This was a moment I'd been living for my entire life and to know that today was the day only made me giddy! I had to run back to the car, because I'd left the door open. Standing there motionless, I took a deep breath, then laughed at myself. When I got to the back-door, Peyton and Karter were coming out. They were so cute. Although they weren't a couple... yet... they looked great together.

After speaking to them and hugging them, I damn near pushed them out the way as they laughed. When I walked in, I saw the man I loved putting icing on the cake. I just stood there staring at him like I hadn't seen him in months. As he finished, he lifted his fingers to his lips to lick the icing off and I had to have cum on myself. When he finally saw me watching him, he smiled. Dropping my bags to the floor I ran to him and practically hopped in his arms as he laughed. His lips were near my ear as he said, "Hey, baby."

My entire body shivered as it often did in his presence. I put my hands to his face and kissed his lips as everyone laughed at me. Once he released me, I began looking for my daughter. "You look amazing."

"Thank you, baby," I said as I continued scanning the front room.

"She's in the bedroom with the therapist and her nurse."

I smiled at him and kissed his lips again, allowing it to linger, then went to greet everyone before making it to Cassie's bedroom. Alana was standing in the doorway with a solemn look on her face and her hand on her chest. When she saw me, she turned to me and met me halfway. "What is it?"

"That little girl is so strong. I don't know where she finds the strength, but when it looks like she's had enough, she musters strength from somewhere and keeps going. I never thought a kid could inspire me, but damn. The tears are threatening to show themselves, so I'm glad you're here."

I smiled at Alana. She hated showing her emotions, which was why she tried to make a joke out of everything or avoid it altogether. When I got to Cassie's doorway, the therapist had just laid her leg on the bed and she was panting as a tear slid down her cheek. "You did so good Cassie. I'm proud of you," the therapist said to her.

The nurse administered some medication, which I immediately wanted to know what it was. When Cassie saw me, her eyes brightened a little although I could still see the weariness in them. "Hi, Mommy."

"Hi, sweetheart."

The nurse explained that she was giving her something for pain and an anti-inflammatory. Once she left Cassie's bedside, I took her spot and leaned over to kiss Cassie. Her head was clammy, and I could imagine why. My poor baby. "I'm glad you're home."

"Me too. I'm glad this is home."

I smiled at her. "Me too. Once you get some rest, I'm gonna get the nurse to help me get you in the tub. We'll wash your hair in there, too. Okay?"

"Okay," she said as she yawned.

I kissed her head again and when I walked down the hallway, Price was coming toward me. "This meal looks amazing. Thank you, baby."

"Thank you for icing the cake."

He pulled me in his arms. "We can both show our gratitude to each other tonight. I think I have blue balls."

I giggled quietly while he frowned. "That's funny, Kendall?"

"No. I'm sorry, baby. After tonight, you shouldn't have that problem anymore."

He pulled me to him and kissed my neck as I moaned softly. When he lifted his head, he stared into my eyes and licked his beautiful lips. "I'm glad to know we here," he said, gesturing his two fingers from my eyes to his.

"Since we're here," I said mimicking his gesture. "Let's go eat, because my stomach is on some other shit right now."

He laughed, then pulled me to the front room. I was already getting used to them being here and it had only been ten minutes. That let me know it was meant to be.

CHAPTER 22

P rice

"She's doing great. I'm watching her and her therapist in the pool, now."

"Indoor, right?"

"Uh... it's like sixty degrees outside. Of course. It's an indoor heated pool."

"Sorry. I know you're taking good care of her. I just wanted to check on her progress. Has she started walking?"

"Yes. Slowly and with a walker but she's walking."

I could hear Shayla sniffing. The moment was really emotional, just knowing how much Cassie had overcome. We'd been home for a month and baby girl was working hard to get back to normal. I was so proud of her. "She's so amazing. How are you? I know it's over-whelming taking care of her."

"It can be, but I'm doing good. I have help. Kendall's mom comes over at least three days a week to help out and so Kendall and I can get some alone time. So, there's only two days a week when Cassie and I are alone for most of the day, besides her nurse and therapist."

"That's good. Well, I have to go. Tell Cassie I called to check on her and that I love her."

"I will."

I ended the call with Shayla. She'd been calling once every other week to check on Cassie's progress. I wasn't quite sure what was going on with her, but I knew she loved Cassie. What she had going on wasn't my business. She'd given up her maternity rights to Cassie, so I was no longer in fear of her changing her mind about the decision she'd made in the hospital. Whenever she called, I answered, though and updated her. Cassie had even gotten to talk to her last time. Cassie didn't seem to be as affected by her absence like she was when Shayla left her with me.

I knew Kendall had a lot to do with that. Kendall had been amazing to the both of us. Although, I wasn't working right now, she took care of me emotionally and knew when I was feeling drained. I cooked mostly, but there were days that she did that, too. Our love had only grown stronger. As soon as Cassie was walking better on her own without the assistance of a walker or cane, I was taking them on vacation. Hopefully, that would be for spring break. If not then, during the summer.

Cassie was still progressing quickly. The only thing that was still healing slowly was her collar bone. That was what was slowing her down. I believe if it had healed before her pelvis and legs, she would be moving even faster than she already was. As her therapist helped her from the pool, I walked over to scoop her up with her towel. "Thank you, Daddy."

"You're welcome, baby."

I brought her to the dressing area, while the therapist stood watch. It was the female dressing room. After helping her dry off, her nurse came in to help her get dressed. I stood outside waiting for her to come out, then we would head home so I could cook. My phone rang before she could come out. It was Kendall. She always called during lunch and her conference period. However, today, she was at the courthouse for West's trial. Had Cassie been doing better, I would have gone with her. Alana and Peyton had gone with her, though. "Hey, baby."

"Hey. Are y'all leaving the pool?"

"In a lil bit. Cassie is getting dressed. How'd it go?"

"Well, West got five years."

That fool deserved more than that and had he been released, he would've suffered the ass whooping I had for him. Karter and I had done research on him and his connection to Tricia and Kendall, but we didn't find anything shady. It was just coincidental that he'd been after the both of them at some point. "Are you happy with that?"

"I guess. It's better than nothing. After his release, he'll have to undergo therapy. That's a stipulation they placed on him."

I could tell she wasn't satisfied with that verdict, but there was nothing we could do about it at this point. "Okay. Are you on your way home?"

"I'm going to a late lunch with Alana and Peyton, then I'll be there."

"Aight, baby. Cassie's coming out, so I'll see you when you get home."

"Okay. I love you."

"Love you, too."

I ended the call and watched my baby girl walk slowly toward me with her walker. She was smiling brightly. She seemed to be moving a little faster than she had been. Her nurse was keeping up with her, just in case she lost her balance. I smiled brightly at her as well. "Look at'chu! You gon' be walking unassisted before you know it."

"I know! Then I can go back to school and play with my friends!"

School was the last thing I was worried about. Kendall had been keeping her current by home-schooling her. Cassie was so smart, that only took like an hour a day. Sometimes, Kendall waited until Saturdays or Sundays and had a three-hour session with her. She didn't have therapy on Sundays, so that session took the place of practically three days. I also didn't want Cassie pushing to get back to school before she was ready. Her injuring herself because she was trying to do too much, would kill me.

After we'd gotten home and I'd gotten dinner prepped, Kendall had arrived. Cassie was out for the count and I was ready to get a pre-celebratory thing popping. When she walked through the door, I grabbed her hand and brought her straight to our bedroom. She dropped her purse and some other information to the floor, then gave me her attention. "Hey," she said softly.

"Hey."

No other words were spoken. I started the shower, then came back to undress her. She bit her bottom lip as I let my hands slide to her back and unzip her dress. Kendall knew that shit got me ready. It was so sexy to watch her tug at her bottom lip with her teeth. Once she did that, it was over. I licked my lips as her dress fell to the floor. Lifting my shirt over my head and dropping my shorts, I realized my shit had sprung loose of my drawers. He was peeping through the pee hole in the front. "Mmm. Let me take care of that for you, baby."

When Kendall went to her knees and pulled off my boxer briefs, I closed my eyes and let my head drop back, because I knew this shit was finna be un-fucking-believable. She'd proven that she could handle a stick shift the old-fashioned way. She didn't just push a button when told to do so. She knew how and when to shift them gears on her own. Watching her pay extra attention to the head was getting me there fast and I couldn't contain myself anymore. I slid it out of her mouth and shot cum all over her chest.

She stood to her feet and I unfastened her bra, then pulled her underwear off. Immediately picking her up, I lowered her to where I needed her most. The groan that escaped me didn't give a shit about being quiet. I couldn't dare wake up Cassie in the other room or this would come to an end before either of us wanted it to. But it seemed when we had to be quiet was when the shit was so fucking good, that feat was impossible.

Kendall wrapped her arms around my neck as I walked to the

shower, holding her steady. Her juices were coating my dick and I could feel them leaking to my balls. She was always so wet for me and I loved it. Once we got in the shower, I began stroking it how she liked it: rough, but slow. Gripping her ass, I began sucking on her beautiful nipples. Kendall was moaning softly. We'd gotten this thing down to a science. Whenever we had time alone, we would probably lose our damn minds.

I allowed her legs to slide from my waist, her feet touching the shower floor and kissed her passionately, taking my time to incite the road to ecstasy. I was a truck driver and I went a lot of places, but this one was my favorite. Pulling away from her slowly and taking her bottom lip part of the way with me, I spun her around and entered her from behind. She was so damn gushy. Maintaining my pace and withholding my nut was always a struggle. Shit, after a few minutes, this nigga was ready to fire one off. Even though I could go multiple rounds, I liked to make sure she was completely satisfied during the first one.

"Price..." she whispered.

"Mmm hmm."

"I'm about to cum."

I pulled out of her and went to my knees, then put my face right in her sweet spot and sucked her clit from the back. When I felt that warm goodness hit my lips, I opened wide to receive that shit with the same gusto in which she gave it. Her body was trembling profusely, and she was fighting to keep her balance. I pulled her to my face, allowing her to rest some of her weight on me as she quenched my thirst, only for it to come right back. We'd both expressed how we would never get enough, and that statement couldn't be more accurate.

When her tremors lessened, I stood to my feet and pushed back inside of her. I rubbed my hand down my mouth, then licked every-thing off it. That was precious, and while I had access to the source, I didn't wanna waste a drop. I picked up my pace as Kendall cursed and swore I was the best dick she ever had. Then, I heard Cassie.

Shit! I loved baby girl, but I wasn't leaving this pussy without leaving my mark. Grabbing Kendall's waist, I pounded that shit until I couldn't stand it anymore. Kendall had stuffed the face towel in her mouth as I slapped her ass twice. I pulled out and nutted all over her back and ass.

We were both panting as I stepped out the shower. "What's up, baby girl?"

"I just wanted you to know I was awake."

"Okay. I'm taking a shower and I'll come check on you in a minute."

I slightly rolled my eyes. I thought she needed me. When I got back to the shower, Kendall was sitting on the bench, trying to catch her breath. She looked up at me and smiled. "That's how you do me?"

"Hell fucking yeah."

"Cassie okay?"

"Yep."

"Well, come do me like that again."

She stood and bent over the bench. After getting my favorite view, she didn't have to convince me of the shit I wanted to do anyway.

If love was a drug, I'd stay high as hell, because Kendall made sure I wanted nothing... that I didn't lack a thing. This woman was the real deal and I knew without a shadow of a doubt that she was the woman I was gonna do life with. While her mama was with Cassie, I came to the jewelry store to pick out a ring. The money that was in savings that I'd been holding to put down on a house had partially made its way to my checking account. Partially because I didn't need all of it, but there was no sense in saving for a house when we were living in a nice house with Kendall.

I went to her bank and paid off the twenty grand she still owed on her mortgage, then came to buy her an engagement ring. We were both all in and had been for months. Cassie and I had been living there with her for over three months now and I just wanted to show her that she wasn't gon' have to wait forever for me to make a move. Because we were already living together, what took some people a good year or longer to know, we knew months ago.

As I perused the ring counter, one caught my attention... finally. Ringing the bell for service, I continued staring at the three-carat beauty. It was a princess cut and had diamonds along the band. It screamed Kendall. When I showed the lady which one I wanted, she lifted her eyebrows. "Someone is extremely special."

"Yeah. Y'all don't have anything in here to do her justice but I'll settle for that one."

She smiled as she handed the ring to me. After looking it over, I pulled the ring from my pocket, and asked her to make it the same size as that one. Kendall had big fingers, so that ring was gon' have to get stretched. While she only wore a women's size ten in clothes, her finger was a size eight, according to the sizing tool the associate used. I dropped six large on that ring, then headed home.

Cassie had been getting along better. She was still using a walker, but she was moving a lot faster. Next week, they would be trying her on a cane. Since she'd been doing so good, I allowed her to stay with Kendall's parents for the weekend. She liked going there, since she was able to get unlimited snacks. Kendall hadn't gotten off work yet and had no idea what was about to happen.

When I got home, I cooked our seafood dinner of shrimp, scallops, oysters, and lobster tail, broccoli, and baked potatoes. I also decided to boil corn on the cob as well. Taking a quick shower and getting dressed, I heard Kendall pulling into the driveway. This was it. Now my nerves were getting the best of me. I had the receipt from the bank and had bought a card to put it in and the ring was in my pocket. I didn't know why I was nervous. She was gonna say yes.

Standing in the middle of the room, I waited for her to walk through the door. The long-sleeved, white, dress shirt I'd worn had proven to be a mistake. I was starting to sweat, and I could feel the perspiration under my arms. My navy dress pants felt tight and my dark brown shoes seemed like they didn't match my belt. I was starting to find so many imperfections, I was about to go change. Before I could make a move to the hallway, Kendall walked through the door. When she looked at me, her steps halted. She glanced around the room and asked, "What's going on?"

I walked toward her and removed her bag from her shoulder and her purse from her hand. When I turned back to her, I could see her eyes were glossy. *Did she already know?* "I just wanna show you some love. Is that okay?"

"Yeah. This is so romantic, Price."

I followed her eyes to the roses on the table and the lit candles. Focusing back on her, I said, "Well, I cooked. Have a seat."

"Where's Cassie?"

"With your parents."

Her eyebrows rose. "Oh, it's gon' be some love, love."

I chuckled. "Yeah, baby. It's gon' be so much love, you ain't gon' be able to walk halfway through it."

"Well, shit. Fuck me up, then."

I chuckled again. She was a mess for real, sometimes. "So, one gift I will give you before dinner and the other will come after."

"Gifts? Why are you giving me gifts?"

"You don't think you deserve them?"

"Hell yeah. But what's the occasion?"

I didn't answer her verbally. Grabbing the envelope from the countertop, I handed it to her as she stared at me. She looked down at it, then back up at me. "You gon' open it?"

She swallowed hard, then tore into it. When she read the card, the tears were sliding down her cheeks. I was thanking her for falling in love with my daughter and loving her like a mother should. Also, how I was glad she was in our lives, giving of herself so unselfishly. Then she looked at the receipt and frowned. "What's this?"

"Look at it."

When realization of what I'd done made it to her face, her mouth opened, and her hand immediately went to it. "Price! You paid off my mortgage?"

I only smiled at her. She jumped from her seat and into my arms as I laughed. "Why did you do this? I can't wait for the next gift. Give it to me now. Please, please, please!"

She was so excited. "I did this because we are living with you. You said that I was your forever, right? That means I ain't going nowhere."

I pulled the box from my pocket and went down on one knee, knowing that she wasn't gonna let me wait until after dinner. Kendall started screaming and jumping up and down, tears falling down her cheeks. "Yes! Yes, Price!"

"But I ain't asked you shit yet!"

I laughed loudly as she calmed down. "Listen." I grabbed her hand and held it in mine. "You are the most beautiful woman I ever laid eyes on. But your heart... damn, girl." I was getting choked up. Looking at the floor, I gathered my composure. "Your heart is even more beautiful. The way you came into our lives to help me with Cassie was just unbelievable. I mean, who does that? Who takes it upon themselves to do as much for Cassie as you did? You did that shit without looking for anything in return."

"But I got you, Price. You and Cassie are the greatest gifts."

"Will you let me finish, woman?"

She giggled, then lifted her hands in surrender. "Thank you."

I playfully rolled my eyes, then continued. "When Cassie got hit by that truck, even though we'd just gotten into it about that fuck nigga, you came to us, to be there for me. One of the most devastating times of my life, you were there for me. And when Shayla did me dirty, you were there. Every time I've needed support, you were there. I'd be a damn fool not to put a ring on your finger. Now, get ready. The question is coming."

She wiped her hand down her face, getting ready. I couldn't help but laugh. "Kendall Washington?"

"Yes?"

"Will you ma..."

She was holding her hand out in my face. I huffed and shook my head slowly, briefly closing my eyes. "Will you do me the honor of being my wife?"

"Yes! God, yes!"

I pulled the ring from the box and slid it on her finger, then stood to my feet. Kendall was in awe, staring at the ring. She looked up at me. "Your words were beautiful. I love you, Price. And I can't wait to spend forever with you."

"I love you, too, sweetheart."

This woman was crazy about me and my daughter. Being with her forever was the main thing on the agenda and it would remain at the forefront of my mind for every decision I made concerning our family. I lowered my head and kissed her, immediately wanting to make love to her, until I heard her stomach growl. "Really, Kendall? You gon' ruin our romantic moment like that?"

"Well, you cooked, and I can smell it and I'm hungry. I can't stop my stomach from growling!"

She slapped my arm as she realized I was fucking with her, as always. I pulled her to me and looked into her eyes for a moment. My lips found hers and I kissed her long, entangling my tongue with hers until her stomach growled again. She started laughing, breaking our kiss. I frowned at her before joining her in laughter. "Shit, girl! Let me feed you before you really ruin the moment."

EPILOGUE

O ne year later...
        Kendall

"The wedding was so beautiful. I just can't believe you guys are married already."

"It seemed like it took forever to get here to me, but we wanted to make sure Cassie was good."

Peyton was looking through our photo album at the destination wedding we'd had this past summer. We'd gone to Bora Bora and had an amazing wedding, only inviting close family and friends. Our honeymoon was in the same location. We'd stayed a week longer than everyone else, although Cassie thought she was staying, too. Price had to burst her bubble. We'd enjoyed one another immensely and more than we ever had.

Cassie and Price had finally had a conversation about him not being her biological father. Shayla had told her the truth while she was in the hospital. She'd told Price that it had made her sad, but that since she was still with him, nothing had changed. Their relationship would never change. I just hoped that as she got older, she wouldn't forget that. I'd seen a girl I'd gone to school with practically disown the man that raised her. To find the man that didn't even know she existed. I prayed that didn't happen with them.

Peyton and Karter were talking about marriage, which was why she was looking through our album. I was beyond happy for her, because she was so in love with Karter. She had her doubts about whether they would ever get to the point that he even wanted to talk about it. He was so hell bent on never getting married again, at first. I'd told Peyton to just be herself and he would get there, especially if he didn't want to lose her.

Peyton and I were a lot alike in that aspect. We both lived to get married and have a family. Alana, not so much. However, P said that she would give Karter eight months to change his mind. After eight months and he still hadn't said anything about it, she decided to bring it up in conversation. She told him how important it was to her and that she couldn't afford to waste time with someone that didn't want the things she did. He made a decision right then, because he said he couldn't afford to lose her. I just prayed like hell that he wasn't leading her on, so she'd stay.

"Where's Cassie now?"

"She's in her room, watching TV. We always wait for Price to get home before we eat dinner."

"Oh okay. Well, let me go, so I won't hold you guys up when he gets here. I'll call you tomorrow."

"Okay, Peyton. Love you, girl."

After we hugged and she left, I took the cupcakes from the oven. I had a little announcement to make and I was gonna use the cupcakes to do so. We'd been trying to get pregnant for the past few months and it just wouldn't happen for us. Finally, I went to see a doctor and he told me that I had a rare condition that would make it hard to get pregnant or even prevent me from conceiving at all. It was an emotional moment for us, especially me. I loved Cassie with all my heart, but I wanted to experience being pregnant and having a baby of my own.

That was all over, though. To my surprise, I missed my cycle two weeks ago. So, I made an appointment with a different doctor that specialized in high risk pregnancies, only for him to confirm that I was indeed pregnant. Not only was I pregnant, but after a vaginal ultrasound he also confirmed that I was having twins. I couldn't be happier. While I knew it may be a hard road ahead, I was ready for it.

Once the cupcakes cooled, I put icing on them and sat them in a platter on the countertop. Not long after, I heard Price in the driveway. He'd started a new job at a different trucking company, but he was also saving money to start his own. I was excited for him and couldn't wait to help him with it. When he came inside, I met him at the door and Cassie came out of her room to greet him as well. "Well, if it isn't my two favorite girls. How was your day?"

"Mine was great, Daddy! I'm starving, though. I'm going wash my hands."

He kissed her cheek, then pulled me to him. "How was your day, beautiful?"

"It was good, baby. Let me fix our food before Cassie dies of hunger."

I kissed his lips and I was so excited, I almost just blurted it out. After fixing their bowls of stew, I sat at the table. Price said grace and we engaged in small talk while I anxiously bounced my leg under the table. I only fixed myself a little because I didn't have much of an appetite. My stomach was sure to get upset if I ate too much. As they finished, I put two cupcakes in front of them. "Oooh, I get two!" Cassie said excitedly.

She loved junk food. The only thing that had changed about her in the last year was her age. Candy, chips, cakes, pies... if it was sweet, she wanted it. I didn't understand how she stayed so slender eating all that. Replacing the junk with fruit had seemed to work, though. I'd much rather her overeat apples, than starburst. She bit into one of the cupcakes and said, "I love strawberry."

It wasn't strawberry. I'd added pink food coloring to one batch and blue food coloring to another. I didn't know what I was having, so I did both. The doctor had said that I was about ten weeks. He was surprised that I wasn't showing yet, being that I was having twins. "Oh, I like strawberry, too."

Price bit into his first cupcake and it was blue. He frowned but kept chewing. Once he'd swallowed, he looked at me. "I was about to say that I didn't like blueberry, but it doesn't taste like blueberry. What is it?"

"It's vanilla. I just used food coloring to get the pink and blue."

Price frowned slightly again as he took another bite. Cassie was content and had finished her cupcake and was working on the second one. Price finished his cupcake and neither of them noticed that I wasn't eating any. After Price licked the icing off his fingers, he looked at me. "You're not eating any? Should I be worried?"

I laughed loudly at his insinuation. "I'm too full right now."

"But you ain't eat that much."

His head tilted to the side. I could tell his brain was working over-time trying to figure out what was going on. Finally, he looked back at me, his eyes wide. Then he shook his head and took a bite of his second cupcake and saw the pink. Hs eyes widened again. Swallowing the bite whole, without chewing, Price said, "I know you aren't trying to tell me what I think you are."

I shrugged my shoulders. "What do you think I'm trying to tell you?"

"You're pregnant?"

I nodded excitedly. Cassie started screaming in excitement. "I'm gonna be a big sister! Finally!"

I laughed as Price stood from his seat and pulled me from mine. "Baby... they were wrong."

"Yes, they were. They were wrong times two."

"Times two?"

"Uh huh. Twins."

Price scooped me up in his arms and practically ran around the house with me, while I screamed. "I'm so damn happy. You happy, Kendall?"

"The happiest I've ever been."

The End

AFTERWORD

From the Author

I love writing about strong men who take care of their children, because I married one. My husband was raising a four-year-old when we met and had been since he was nine months old. So, this book was somewhat reflective for me. I hope that you enjoyed the story.

There's also an amazing playlist on iTunes for this book under the same title that includes some great R&B and rap tracks to tickle your fancy. Please keep up with me on Facebook (@authormonicawalters), Instagram (@authormonicawalters) and Twitter (@monlwalters). You can also visit my Amazon author page at www.amazon.com/author/monica.walters to view my releases. Also, subscribe to my webpage for updates! https://authormonicawalters.wixsite.com/mysite.

For live discussions, giveaways and inside information on upcoming releases, join my Facebook group, Monica's Romantic Sweet Spot at https://bit.ly/2P2lo6X.

Coming up:

Please register to meet me, and some amazing authors, on

October 5, 2019 at the Houston Loves Books event at www. houstonlovesbooks.com! Paperbacks will be on deck and waiting to be signed, just for you.

I will also be in Memphis November 2-3, 2019 for BLP's first meet and greet! Come meet the #girlgang at the BLP Winter Wonderland! Register at Bit.ly/BLPWW19. We look forward to seeing you there!

Sweet Misery

Sweet Exhale